Light of Mine

Book One of the Towers of Light Series

Allen Brokken

"Let your light so shine before men, that they may see your good works, and glorify your Father which is in heaven."
Matthew 5:16

Light of Mine
Book One: The Towers of Light series
Copyright © 2019-2022 Allen Brokken

Written by Allen Brokken
Edited by Sarah Grimm
Cover Design by Magpie Designs, Ltd
Photo Credit: Imgorthand
Texture Credit: Sascha Duensing
Edition 5.7
ISBN: 978-1-7378515-0-9

Dedication

To my mom for always encouraging my writing, including the epic hundred-page handwritten story she typed for me in 6th grade.

To my dad, for being the hardest-working person, I have ever known. Without his example, this would have never become real.

To my big brother for building my first fort with me, which inspired building the Tower of Light for my children.

To my little brother, for our adventures in that first fort.

To my wife for allowing me to have the real-life adventures that drove me to write this story and for her ongoing encouragement to finish it.

To my children, for the inspiration to write the story and for their feedback and support through the whole process.

To Tammy for volunteering her grammar skills to help me finalize this book, without which I would have never dared to bring it to print.

To Amy and Sara, who each inspired me without realizing it to take this book over the finish line.

To Patti and Angie for transforming the second edition into the real novel it is now.

To Anna and Daniel for their artistry.

To Jason and Brice for workshopping through this book with me for over a year to make it better.

To Brandon and Brandon for sharing their literary genius and tricks of the trade freely with the public.

To the Realm Makers for showing me the way.

To Sarah for teaching me about conflict and suspense.

Contents

1.   The Tower of Light

Father nearly flattened Lauren as he blundered through the kitchen door with an awkward bundle of rolled parchment. Lauren dodged out of Father's way and managed not to drop her brother's dirty dishes. Ever since she turned twelve, Mother had given her more and more responsibility. She knew Mother would be proud of her fancy footwork, saving the dishes from certain destruction.

"Aiden, clear the table, please," Father said with his commanding but warm voice.

Aiden, the family's middle child, complied by grabbing the side of the cast iron spider pot from the center of the table and pulling it to him. Lauren watched him strain with it, then wrap it up in a bear hug to carry it, which was apparently a bit much for his nine-year-old frame. She stepped over and attempted to help him.

"I can do it, Sissy!" Aiden barked at her as he adjusted the weight. Mother wasn't going to be happy if he got soot from the sides of the pot all over his plaid cotton shirt and khaki pants. But Lauren wasn't going to start an argument over it in front of Father.

"OK, OK. You can handle it, but why don't you actually *handle* it?" Lauren pointed to the pot's heavy wire handle.

"Oh," Aiden replied sheepishly, then set the pot on the floor and used both hands to grab the wire. He could manage it that way much better, so she turned her attention to Father.

Father unrolled and flattened the parchment to reveal building plans and then sat down in his rough-hewn

1

armchair at the head of the table. Father put his left hand over his mouth and leaned in to rest his elbow on the table. His weathered fingers nearly covered his nearly white goatee.

Lauren glanced at the plans herself, realizing that it outlined some kind of fortification. She returned to her task of washing the dishes. *Why would Father be working on defenses at home? Was the Darkness loose on the Heathlands?*

Lauren dried the plate she had just washed and turned to put it on the counter. As she worked, she saw Father sit back and rub his face. He must have been lost in thought because he jumped in his chair as five-year-old Ethan hopped onto his lap and asked, "What's this, Daddy?"

His red hair was a tousled mess as Mother was loath to cut his curly locks, so Father had to adjust the boy on his lap to still see the plans.

Aiden climbed into the chair next to him and leaned over the table, mimicking the pose Father had displayed just a moment ago. "It looks like a tower to heaven!"

Father rubbed the top of Aiden's head, pushing back his short-cropped blond hair, and smiled as Aiden turned to look at him. "You are close, my son. It's a lighthouse."

"A lighthouse?" Lauren couldn't concentrate on her task any longer, so she wiped her hands on a white apron that covered her pale blue paisley work dress and took a ribbon out of its pocket. She tied back her sandy-brown hair as she bent over the table to look at the plans. They showed three different cross-sectional views of a wooden structure with various lines indicating size measurements.

Mother came through the door with a wooden milk bucket in one hand, startling everyone from their study of the plans. She was careful not to spill any milk on her pale blue dress as she put the bucket on the counter, then joined the rest of the family by the table.

Mother rested her hand on Father's shoulder, and Lauren noticed Father wince slightly as he looked up into Mother's brown eyes. Something about that look told Lauren bad news was coming. A wave of anxiety went through Lauren and settled as a tight knot in her stomach.

"Have you told them what it's for?" Mother asked with a frown.

"There's no ocean for hundreds of miles," Lauren interjected. "What would a lighthouse be guiding to safety?"

"Children, I didn't know how to tell you this," Father spoke in a halting manner. "I'm going away for a while."

"What?" Lauren gasped.

Ethan began to cry.

"Where are you going, Daddy?" Aiden asked with a hint of fear in his voice. "To Grandma's house?"

"No, son." Father put his arm around Ethan and kissed the crying boy on the top of his head. "I'm traveling to Blooming Glen and other places on the outskirts of the Heathlands."

"Isn't that where the Darkness is?" Lauren wrung her hands.

"No, Daddy, don't leave!" Ethan buried his head in Father's chest.

Aiden jumped out of his seat and wrapped one arm around Ethan, the other around Father, then hid his face in Father's shoulder.

"Not yet. At least that's the hope." Father patted Aiden's back. "You know I finished my studies last month. I'm now a Master Artificer, and I can craft all kinds of arms and defenses against the Darkness. I'm to help the Mighty Mercenaries defend the battlefront."

"I know the Mighty Mercenaries are supposed to be the most valiant warriors in Zoura. But if the Darkness falls before you can set up the new defenses, won't it get you, too?" Lauren asked. At this, Mother came over and put an arm around Lauren's shoulder. Lauren looked up and saw tears streaming from the corners of her mother's dark brown eyes.

"That's why we'll build this tower here on our farm. As long as the Light shines on me, I will always be safe from the Dark One, and no matter how the Darkness spreads, I will find my way home." Father took his hand off Ethan's back and leaned closer to the table to point at the symbol of a lantern at the top of the tower.

Ethan wiped his eyes and looked at the plans again. "Daddy, can I help build? I want to keep you safe from the Darkness."

At that, tears began to pool at the corners of Father's eyes. "Of course, son. In fact, you all can help."

Aiden let go of Father, took a deep breath, and composed himself. "I'm a good builder. I can help too. What are we going to build it with?"

"Cedar," Father said. "It's practical and grows right here."

Despite the change in subject, Lauren still worried about Father being lost to the Darkness. The tales of what happened to people under the Darkness were terrifying: untreatable diseases killing whole towns, dark creatures intent on murder roaming the streets, and people being forced to do the Dark One's bidding. She didn't want one of those horrible ends for her daddy. However, she saw her brothers being brave, so she decided to put on a good face for now. She tried to come up with something positive to say, then remembered the cedar chest in which her best dress was stored. "And cedar wood smells good." The comment didn't cheer Lauren as she'd hoped.

***

For the next few weeks, Lauren woke at dawn, determined to help Father in any way she could to keep him safe from the Darkness. She wasn't sure how the tower would really help if he were in a faraway land, but Father had said so, and he was very wise, so she focused on helping Father by carrying supplies, holding boards while Father cut or nailed them, or fetching water when he got hot. The business helped Lauren take her mind off her anxiety and worries.

While Father did most of the work, with Lauren a close second, Aiden was good at following the plans to lay out supplies for the next piece of work, and Ethan could fetch things like nails when they ran out. Mother kept up with the normal chores, making sure they all had plenty to eat and drink.

As the second story of the Tower began to take shape, Lauren helped Father put in the stairs. She sat on a lower step and held the pleasant-smelling cedar planks in place as Father nailed the plank into the frame with square-topped iron nails. It was precarious work as Father was perched on a ladder that leaned against the steps. When he finished, he reached into his tool belt for more nails while Lauren put the next plank in place.

"Ethan," Father called with his deep, commanding voice. After a moment's pause, he called again more forcefully, "Ethan!"

The boy popped his head into the open doorway at the bottom of the tower. "Yes, Daddy?"

"I'm almost out of nails. Can you bring a bag up to me?"

"Daddy, they're heavy. I'm too little." Ethan whined.

"Ethan, I'll never assign a task you can't do. You bear the Light, son. Right now, I need you to shine that light by obeying and doing something hard. Can you do that for me?" Father replied, his voice level and compassionate.

"OK, Daddy, I'll do it," Ethan replied as he shuffled out of the Tower.

Father's words to Ethan touched Lauren deeply. "Daddy, is that why you're going away? Did God ask you to do something hard to shine your light?"

Father hung the hickory-handled claw hammer from his belt and put a leather-clad hand on Lauren's shoulder. She looked up into her father's eyes and saw tears welling in the corners. This cut deep into Lauren's heart; Daddy never cried.

"Yes, Lauren, the Lord put a heavy burden on my heart to make sure the Light shines in faraway places. I want more than anything to stay here with the family. Mother would go with me to help…she's much more than just a prayer warrior, but it's not safe for you children to come along. The Lord has asked me to do the hard thing, so I must." Father wiped his eyes with the back of his glove.

At this, Lauren began to cry as well. "But, Daddy, who will keep us safe?"

Father took off his glove and put it in his tool belt, then reached into his pants pocket and pulled out his handkerchief. He used it to wipe the tears from Lauren's face.

"Daddy! Help! Help!" Ethan cried from outside the tower.

This startled Father, and he suddenly turned toward the door. The movement knocked the ladder out of balance, and Father flailed to try to keep it in place. Lauren grabbed for the ladder to pull it back but missed, and it fell away from the steps and into the opposite wall of the tower.

Father's head banged against the wall. Lauren saw him hang from one arm for an instant. Then he lost his grip and fell to the floor.

"Daddy!" Lauren cried as she rushed down the completed stairs. She jumped off the last three steps and dashed to Father's side.

"Daddy! Help!" Ethan called again as he stepped into the tower.

"Ethan! You scared Daddy! Look what you did!" Lauren turned to glower at her brother and pointed accusingly at where Father was slumped on the floor, shaking his head and rubbing the back of it. "But there's a frog on my noggin! Help!" Ethan pointed to the top of his head.

Lauren did a double-take. On top of Ethan's curly mess of red hair was a rainbow-striped bullfrog. The colorful frog sparkled in the light coming in from the open doorway. She had never seen anything like it.

"Come here, Ethan. Let me see this frog," Father said shakily from behind Lauren. She turned and saw Father pull himself up to a sitting position and lean against the wall.

"Oh, Daddy!" Ethan said as he came to kneel next to Father. He reached up to touch the bump on the back of Father's head. "I gave you a head egg! I'm sorry!"

Father appeared to be in a daze as he focused on the frog on Ethan's head for what felt like an eternity.

"Daddy, are you OK?" Lauren asked, worried that he might have really been hurt in the fall.

Father shook his head as if to clear it. "Do you know what kind of frog that is?"

"Daddy, you just took a bad fall. Is this really time for a nature lesson?" Lauren had concern in her voice.

"Yeah, Daddy, can you please get it off my head?" Ethan replied.

Father sat up straighter. "It's a Zourian Flying Frog. I've never seen one outside of a drawing in a book. It is said they are touched by the Light."

Father took the frog from Ethan's head and put it on the bump on his own head. Light sparkled all around the frog, and the swelling on Father's head disappeared.

Ethan clapped his hands. "Daddy! He fixed your head egg!"

Father looked deeply into Lauren's eyes. "You asked who will keep you safe. The Lord provides for those dedicated to the Light."

Lauren nodded, amazed at the miracle she had just witnessed.

"Can we keep him, Daddy?" Ethan asked, pointing at the frog proudly perched on Father's head.

"I'm pretty sure the frog has chosen to keep us, son," Father replied as he gingerly removed the frog from its perch.

"Oh, goodie, goodie! I'll call him Sparkle Frog." Ethan reached for the frog, and Father gave it to him.

"Ethan, why don't you take your new friend down to the creek for a swim?" Father said with a big smile as he began to rise.

"Are you sure you should get up, Daddy?" Lauren asked. "I can go get Mamma."

Father stood up carefully and pushed the ladder above him back into place. "Never felt better. Sparkle Frog was miraculous. Let's go get some water, and we'll tell Mother and Aiden about our new friend."

***

A few weeks later, in May of that year, the three-story tower was complete. It had a peaked roof and shuttered windows; its bottom two stories were enclosed with wooden logs. On the Sabbath, after the tower was finished, Father asked the parson to come for dinner. Lauren really liked the parson, who was kind to her, answering any question she might have, so she was glad to have him. Also, he occasionally gave the siblings sweet treats. The clergyman, in his forties, wore simple, white linen clothes with a cross pin on his right lapel. Lauren didn't know how he kept them so clean; Mother only let her wear her white dress to church on the Sabbath, and then she had to change it as soon as she got home. *How did the parson keep his clothes so clean?*

Mother led the parson to the table, and he set the burlap sack he was carrying underneath the table before taking his seat.

After a delicious meal of Mother's fried chicken, mashed potatoes, green beans, and biscuits, the parson wiped his mouth and said, "Children, your father tells me you are more diligent than the ants of the field. You have built a solid tower in record time."

"Thank you, sir!" exclaimed the children.

The parson rose from the table. "There is just one thing missing."

"What?" asked Ethan, echoing what Lauren was thinking. Father's plans were so detailed. She couldn't imagine what they'd missed.

The parson bent over and picked up his sack, then removed a metal lantern and set it on the table. "The Light, of course."

The lantern was a dull bronze color that reminded Lauren of the brass knockers on the church door. It looked about five hands high and one hand wide. The glass faces had a golden stained-glass cross in the center of each face. She really loved that because it reminded her of the stained-glass window in her grandma's great room. The lantern held no candle, but a small spike protruded from its center.

Aiden set his elbows on the table and leaned closer. "Mama, will you get a candle, so we can light it?"

The parson patted Aiden on the head. "Son, not for this lantern."

Ethan looked at the parson with a puzzled look on his face. "What does it use?"

Father pointed at Ethan's chest. "The light for this lantern is inside of each of us. "

Ethan's chin went down, then up, and he threw his hands into the air. "I don't see the light, Daddy."

"When you love the Lord with all your heart, mind, and spirit, the Good Book says you reflect the Savior's Light on the world, which pushes back the Darkness." Father scooted his chair close to Ethan and patted his head. "Would you like to learn a song about how we can shine that light?"

Ethan clapped his hands. "Oh, that sounds fun, Daddy."

Father got up from his chair and moved the lantern to the center of the table. "We all can sing. I think Lauren and Aiden know the song already."

Father knelt next to Ethan and held up his index finger. "This little light of mine," he began. "I'm gonna let it shine."

For a moment, Lauren thought it was silly to sing this little kids' song in front of the parson. After all, she was twelve years old. However, she was overtaken by her brother's excitement and joined in.

Soon everyone, including the parson, joined in. As they sang the song, the tip of the spike in the lantern began to shine. The longer they sang, the more its radiance increased. By the second verse, about not hiding the light, it glowed as brightly as a Christmas candle.

As they finished with "Shine it all over the whole wide world. I'm gonna let it shine," a bright blue-white flame engulfed the spike. The radiance filled the inside of the lamp so brilliantly, and it lit the entire house. Lauren was filled with joy and hope. Daddy would be protected by the Light despite his travels into distant lands.

Father picked up the lantern. "Children, as long as we stay faithful to the Lord, this Light will shine over the Heathlands. We must do our work the very best we can as if for the Lord. We must pray, read the Good Book, and honor the Sabbath. We must pay heed to even little things, like watering the animals or cleaning up after dinner. We must do our work obediently, with a happy heart, and the Light will always shine."

Father carried the lantern to the top of the tower and set it in place. Its light shone out over the Heathlands as if it were intent on banishing the Darkness wherever it threatened to reach.

The next morning, Father left on his mission to help the Mighty Mercenaries defend the Heathlands against the Darkness.

Lauren was determined that no matter what, she would keep the Light shining so he would come home safely.

2.   Tragedy Strikes

Two months later

Late in the evening, a storm raged with terrible winds and rain. Thunder boomed, and lightning crashed outside the small cabin, keeping Mother awake with fear for her children's safety, especially since Father was still gone. Mother kept vigil in the great room, initially comforted by the Light from the tower shining through the window. However, as the storm grew in intensity, the wind blew so fiercely that the lantern looked as if it would blow out of the Tower of Light. Mother was so concerned about losing the lamp and its holy fire that she battled through the rain to get to the tower and close the shutters.

As soon as the shutters were closed, she heard a deafening boom of thunder that shook the top of the tower, followed by a loud crash. She raced down the stairs to see what had happened. With the shutters on the tower closed and the storm raging overhead, she could barely see her hands in front of her face. She decided it would be better to investigate in the morning and ran through the rain back to the house. The whole incident left her even more unsettled, and she tossed and turned through the night.

***

The next morning, Aiden woke up to the unfamiliar sound of a kitten crying, "Meow. Meow," from across the room. He sat up in bed, crinkling the hay-stuffed mattress, and saw Lauren standing across the room, putting a kitten in the right front pocket of her linen paisley work dress. The kitten looked out over the top of the pocket and wiggled its white-tipped black ears, and cried, "Meow. Meow."

"Sissy, where'd the kitten come from?" Aiden asked after her as she turned to go down the stairs.

Lauren stopped cold. "Kitten, what kitten?" She looked over her shoulder at Aiden.

"Meow. Meow," came the muffled cry from the kitten in her pocket.

"The one in your pocket, Sissy." Aiden hopped out of the bed he shared with Ethan.

Lauren put her index finger to her lips. "Shhh. I don't know where he came from, and I don't know what Mama would think about a kitten staying in the loft."

"She let E keep Sparkle Frog, and I got to keep Daddy Duck." Aiden's reply was matter of fact.

"But they don't come in the house. You know how Mama can be about animals in the house," Lauren whispered conspiratorially.

Aiden's eyes bored into Lauren's as he rebuked her. "You need to tell Mama! Keeping secrets about something you think might be wrong helps the Darkness. With Daddy gone, we have to keep the Light strong."

She pulled the kitten out of her pocket and held him. "You're right. I will. But he's sooo cute and so little, he can't live on his own. Look at him."

"He is little. I'm surprised he's away from his mother." Aiden stroked the kitten's back. "You're such a little guy. How did you ever get up here?"

"Meow, meow," the kitten replied as if he were answering Aiden's question.

Aiden took the kitten from Lauren and looked him in the eyes. "I didn't understand your answer, little one. How about I give you a simpler question? What's your name?"

The kitten replied authoritatively, "Meow, meow."

Lauren took the kitten back. "Well, I guess that settles it. Not the most original name, but I like it. Meow-Meow it is." Then she put him in her pocket and climbed down the ladder from the loft to the great room.

Aiden looked down at Lauren and Meow-Meow. How did that tiny kitten get all the way upstairs? Lauren always wanted a kitten; maybe Mother gave it to her as a surprise.

Aiden followed Lauren into the kitchen, expecting Lauren to talk to Mother about the kitten. When he got there, he was surprised to see Mother carrying two buckets of water into the house. "Mama, what's going on? Daddy built the windmill for that."

Lauren rushed over to help with the buckets. However, Mother just set the buckets on the thick oak counter next to the five-gallon ceramic water crock.

"Last night, the storm knocked the blades off the windmill." Mother turned toward the fireplace and took her patchwork apron off its hook, and tied it over her white linen shirt and gray wool skirt. "I used the last of what was in the reservoir to fill the animals' troughs. We'll have to get water the old-fashioned way until Daddy comes home."

Aiden ran to the window to look at the windmill. "I can fix it, Mama."

"I'm sure you can." Mother smiled as she wiped the sweat from her brow and then tied back her shoulder-length brown hair with a ribbon. "However, the windmill is very tall. Better wait till Father is here to help."

"OK, Mama." Aiden's shoulders slumped as he walked over to the table and took a seat on a three-legged stool. He longed to be the man in the house, but no one could replace Father.

"Lauren." With her most stern voice, Mother addressed Lauren. "What's in your pocket?"

Lauren stopped cold. Aiden could sense she was anxious that she wouldn't be able to keep the kitten. He got up and put his hand on Lauren's shoulder, which was awkward since she was a head taller. He really wasn't sure how Mother would react to Lauren's new friend, but he'd stand with Sissy. Besides, he'd love a new pet.

Lauren reached into her pocket and carefully pulled out Meow-Meow. "A kitten?" she said sheepishly.

"Oh, how precious. Where did you find such a tiny thing?" Mother asked as she came closer for a look.

"He was in my bed this morning. I can't figure out how he could have gotten there. Can I keep him?" Lauren handed the kitten to Mother.

Mother rubbed his fur against the grain and looked him all over. "I don't know how he got there, either, but he doesn't seem to have any fleas or lice, so you can keep him. Does your new friend have a name?"

"I called him Meow-Meow," Lauren replied with a sigh. Aiden let out his own sigh of relief. He hated to admit it, but he thought the kitten was cute, too.

As Lauren put the kitten back into her pocket, Ethan dragged his feet through the door from the great room. "I want oaka-meal, Mama."

Aiden stifled a laugh at his brother's expense because his red hair was particularly obnoxious this morning. He wondered if Mother would ever cut his hair to a proper length like his own short-cropped blond hair.

Aiden's contemplations were interrupted by grumbling in his own stomach. He turned to Mother as she poured water out of a bucket and into a cast-iron spider pot, then added two cups of steel-cut oats. "Getting the water put me behind today, Sweet Pea. The fire has just died down enough so I can cook. It will be about an hour before breakfast is ready."

Mother put the spider pot in the fireplace. "Carrying all that water has me winded, plus I'm out of practice. All of your father's inventions have made life too easy, I guess." She scooped hot coals from the fire with a small shovel and placed them over the spider pot. "While we wait, I'll get started with Ethan's lessons."

"Lessons! But I'm hungry!" Ethan pouted.

"We're all hungry. We'll have food soon enough." Mother set the shovel down and then wiped her hands on her apron. "Lauren, do you think you could do the milking on your own?"

"Yes, Mama." Lauren set down the patchwork apron she'd picked up after she came down from the loft. She could tell Mama was tired from getting the water, so she was happy to help.

"I'll gather the eggs, Mama." Aiden grabbed the egg basket.

"I'm so grateful that you all took to heart Father's admonition to shine the Light in daily activities," Mother said as she gave each child a hug. She went into the great room and came back with a writing slate and chalk, then sat at the kitchen table with Ethan.

17

As Lauren walked to the barn, Aiden rushed past her on his mission to gather the eggs. On his way, he noticed the sky was unusually overcast in a way he hadn't seen since before they built the tower. Aiden was always curious about the weather, so he wondered if that meant there would be another thunderstorm this morning. His thoughts were interrupted when he noticed windmill blades mired in the mud next to the flat limestone path between the house and the barn.

Aiden hurried forward to inspect the blades. The shaft appeared to have melted. He remembered hearing a gigantic thunderclap last night. It was the loudest thunder he had ever heard, and it had shaken the house. He was terrified and wanted Daddy to be home. Had the windmill been struck by lightning?

After poking at the shaft's molten edges, Aiden remembered his mission to gather the eggs and decided he should talk to Mama about the melted metal on the windmill blades later. Then he ran off to the chicken coop to finish his chore.

As he unhooked the latch on the coop, he looked back and saw Lauren trying to hopscotch across the limestone blocks between the house and the barn. He shook his head as he thought about how girls were always trying to keep clean and proper. He looked down at his now very muddy bare feet and wiggled his toes in the mud, and thought about how much he liked the mud squishing between them.

Then he caught sight of a monster earthworm right by his big toe. He reached down and pulled it free of the mud and let it wriggle around in his open palm. It was the biggest nightcrawler he'd ever seen. He knew exactly who was going to get this prize…if he was around.

"Daddy Duck! Daddy Duck!" he called, though the duck didn't always respond. "Here, boy, I've got a treat for you." Wanting to see his special animal friend, Aiden began to wave the worm around in the air.

He suddenly heard a familiar "quack" as he felt the whoosh of flapping wings and a tug on the worm. He let go of his bait and saw the golden duck fly off toward the creek.

A sense of dread tightened Aiden's stomach. Something was very wrong. Ever since the Tower had been built, there was an almost blinding flash of light every time Daddy Duck came around. Today, no flash occurred. He searched his mind for reasons why. Had the Dark One done something to Daddy Duck? He needed to talk to Mama. This could be bad.

Aiden was so concerned that he ran out of the chicken coop without locking it up. Then he saw the windmill parts on the ground and realized the blades were shiny themselves, or maybe it was just the combination of the tower and the windmill blades. With the windmill broken, there was no light from Daddy Duck.

Aiden heard a clucking noise behind him and realized that he had left the chicken coop open. He raced back and shooed the chickens back into the coop, and then he proceeded to feed them. He could talk to Mama about the windmill when he got done.

***

Aiden returned to the kitchen with his basket of eggs. "Mama, did you see the windmill blades on the ground?"

"I saw them. It explains why the sink isn't working, and that must have been the crash I heard last night." Mother retrieved a cast iron skillet from its hook and put a dollop of lard in the middle of it.

"It looks like lightning struck it." Aiden wiped off the eggs with a damp cloth. Lauren had already returned from her chore and came over to help him.

"Lightning, you say. How do you know that?" Mama put the skillet on a rack in the fireplace to heat up.

"It was melted like it would be if the blacksmith put it on the forge. Daddy once said lightning could do that." Aiden pointed out the window at the top of the barn. "Daddy told me we have lightning rods to protect us from lightning strikes like this. He said lightning could start fires if you aren't careful. He also said it always hits the highest spot."

Aiden took Mother's hand and pulled her to the window, with Lauren following them. "But the windmill isn't the highest spot. Do you think the Dark One did it, Mama? Did he destroy the windmill with lightning?"

"It's possible, I guess. It was a powerful storm. What do you think the Dark One would gain by breaking our windmill?" Mama grabbed the skillet with a hot pad and set it on the counter. She cracked eggs into the pan with the melted lard.

"Maybe just to make our lives harder?" Aiden sat down at the table. "Daddy said that the Dark One likes to get people to fight and grumble during hardships. That makes their light weaker."

"You are right about the Dark One trying to weaken us, but I know our faith is powerful." Mother put the skillet back on the fire and began to fry the eggs. "A few extra chores aren't going to dim the Light you children reflect on the world, right?"

"No, ma'am." Their answer rang with youthful confidence.

"Then maybe it's something else. Daddy Duck flew to me today, and he didn't flash." Aiden added.

"Didn't flash; what do you mean?" Mother asked as she flipped the eggs.

"Ever since we put the lantern in the tower, Daddy Duck seems to flash a bright light when he's flying toward you, but today he didn't flash," Aiden explained as he watched Mother finish breakfast.

"Oh, that is concerning." Mother put eggs on a plate. "When the duck wandered onto the property, your father said the way he never lost his golden baby feathers showed he was marked by the Light. But Father was never really sure what that meant."

Aiden was now very worried about the change to his duck. *What other changes had happened on the farm that they hadn't noticed? Did Meow-Meow's coming relate to the Light as well?*

He was about to ask when he heard the sloppy clip-clop of horse hooves in the yard. *Who could be coming to visit at this hour?*

"Children, I wasn't expecting anyone this morning," Mother said as she hurried to take the skillet off the fire and then pull the spider pot out of the stove. "I'm not sure the oatmeal is completely done, but I don't want to risk it burning."

21

Mother rushed the pot to the middle of the table and set it on a clay trivet. Lauren followed her lead with the plate of eggs. "You read my mind, Lauren. Get the plates and feed the boys. I'll go see who this is."

A loud knock sounded on the front door. Mother hurried from the kitchen into the great room. Aiden peeked around the door frame from the kitchen and saw Mother look out the small window in the center of the door. She took a step back and opened the door.

From his vantage point, Aiden saw just outside the door a huge man who wore the armor of the Mighty Mercenaries in the colors of Father's cadre. The man was completely caked with mud, and the color of his uniform seemed muted. The man had a large burlap sack full of something bulky slung over his back. Aiden was concerned about a stranger appearing unexpectedly, but he looked like he was in Father's unit. Maybe he was a messenger sent by Father.

"Please come in, sir." Mother stepped back and allowed the burly man to enter the great room. He looked around for a minute, then set the big sack next to the coat tree behind the door. The wool winter cloaks hanging from the tree obscured it from further view.

"Name's Wrothdar, ma'am; no need for formalities." The man looked at his feet and shuffled from side to side. "No good way to say this, but by all accounts, we've lost your husband, ma'am."

"You've lost my husband?" Mother stated flatly. Aiden watched as she stood stock-still for what seemed an eternity.

Mother's face reddened, "What does that even mean?" she yelled as she got right up in his face despite their height difference.

The big man took two steps back, which landed him on the porch again. "Well, ma'am, we got hit by the fiercest storm we ever saw up by Clark's Ford. Night watch didn't see what happened, but his tent was just gone when the storm let up."

Mother took deep breaths and stepped back from the big man into the great room. She looked like she was trying to compose herself. Despite that, Aiden was starting to get scared. What was he saying about Father?

"We think the storm washed him away in a flash flood. We set out right away looking, and we found his weapons and armor all washed up on the shore a little way downstream. I've been ridin' all night to get here." Wrothdar stepped back into the house and continued with a forlorn expression. "Given the storm, we're not holding out any hope. He's a goner, ma'am."

"No! You're lying! Get out, you liar! Get out of my house!" Mother yelled powerfully as she rushed forward and shoved the man in the chest. Aiden had never seen Mother like this before.

Now Ethan and Lauren joined him at the doorway. Mother closed the gap between herself and the big man and began pounding on his chest, pushing him with such ferocity that he backed out of the house and stood just outside. "My husband isn't a goner!" Mother shouted from just inside the doorway, "If he was, I'd know it. The Light is still glowing in the tower, so he is not dead!"

As if for confirmation, she looked up at the tower. "No! The shutters!" Mother cried. "I left the shutters closed after the storm!" Mother rushed out the front door, leaving it wide open. Lauren and Ethan followed as Aiden snuck into the great room, and they watched out the door as Mother ran past the big man on the porch. Aiden saw her disappear into the bottom of the tower and re-emerge moments later from the top as she began opening the shutters.

Light streamed out of the tower as if a dam had broken. It flowed down the tower across their farm and then washed over the Heathlands. Despite the overcast sky, everything suddenly looked as if it were noontime on a sunny day. Bathed in the glow from the Tower of Light, even the mud on Wrothdar's armor seemed less filthy.

The children continued to watch the dumbstruck warrior as Mother returned to the porch. "That's my husband's horse, correct?" she asked. Aiden thought her voice sounded flat, like when he did something naughty, and she was trying not to yell at him.

"Yes, ma'am," Wrothdar stammered.

Mother pointed at Wrothdar, her mind made up. "Tie up the horse and go; I have important things to take care of. Tell your leaders my husband is not dead, and they had better keep looking for him. The safety of the Heathlands depends on his return."

The big man merely nodded and did as he was told. Mother came back into the great room.

Lauren stepped forward. "What is happening, Mama? Why did that man come here?"

Mother cleared her throat and took a couple of deep breaths. "Lauren, sweetie, something has happened to

Daddy. The soldier who just came brought awful news, but he's either wrong or, worse yet, he's lying."

Mother put her arms around the children and ushered them toward the kitchen. "This is all very upsetting, especially on an empty stomach. Let's get some food in us."

Mother settled them at the table and doled out oatmeal and eggs to each of the children. Aiden was too shocked by it all to say a word. Then Mother did something unusual. She cut two pieces of bread and put her eggs in between them, and wrapped that up in a kitchen towel. "I know your Daddy is still alive, and I think Fleetfoot can help me find him."

Mother hurried to the kitchen counter and packed provisions in an empty flour sack. "The soldiers don't understand. They are not all followers of God like we are. I doubt they will be looking in the right places or searching for the right signs. Daddy needs me. I'm sorry, but I must go."

Aiden felt the warmth leave his body as he was gripped by fear. Father was already gone; the soldier said he was a goner. Did the big man think Daddy was dead? Now Mama was going to leave. Who would take care of them?

Mother stopped packing, came over to the table, and put her hands on Lauren's shoulders. "Lauren, sweetie, I have to ask you to do something very hard. While I am gone, you must watch over the boys." With a bittersweet look on her face, Mother stroked Lauren's hair. "Clark's Ford will be a day there and back and maybe a day of searching."

"Mama, what are you saying?" Lauren asked as she turned to look at her mother. Aiden had never seen Lauren look so scared.

"Before you children were born, your father and I fought the Darkness together. I have to go help him now. I need you to make sure you and the boys are fed while I'm gone." Mother stroked Laurens's hair as she looked into her eyes. "I just baked bread, which should make a couple of meals. There are cut oats for a few meals, and the last of the salted pork is in the smokehouse. You know about the eggs and the milk."

Then Mother squatted down and pulled Lauren into a loving embrace. "Father was supposed to be bringing home some supplies to get us to harvest, so you'll have to be careful with what you have. Can you do that?"

Lauren nodded almost imperceptibly in response to Mother's orders.

Mother looked into Lauren's eyes. "I won't be gone for more than a couple of days and will bring more supplies when I come. God willing, I'll bring Daddy back with me." Mother stood up and stepped away from Lauren. "Boys, come here."

The boys rushed from their seats and hugged their mother.

"Boys, Lauren is in charge while I'm gone." Her voice rang clear and calm, though tears filled her eyes. "You don't need to be scared; the Light of Truth will protect you. You all are very special, and I love you very much."

Mother squatted down to their level as if to emphasize the gravity of what she was about to say. "Watch out for each other and keep one another safe. Please do your chores and stick to your regular routine. If you need help, go to the parson. I'll tell him what happened as I leave. He will send helpers. You will see."

Mother held them for a moment and said, "No matter what, make sure the Light stays shining in the tower."

"I'll keep the Light shining, Mama!" Ethan declared with tears in his eyes.

"Us, too," chimed Lauren and Aiden. Aiden hugged Mother extra tight.

Mother paused for what seemed an eternity, then gently broke their embrace. She took the sack of provisions, and the children followed her into the great room as she picked up her small black leather-bound copy of the Good Book from its place next to her rocking chair. Then she left through the door without looking back.

Aiden saw her put the supplies in Fleetfoot's saddle bag and pull herself onto the horse's back. Then with tears streaming down her face, she waved and set off at a fast pace.

At first, Lauren and Ethan were frozen in shock, just like Aiden was. Then a sob escaped Aiden's throat. How could they protect the Light when he wasn't sure how they would even feed themselves without Mother? And what had happened to Father? Was he ever going to come home?

Lauren and Ethan surely were wondering the same things as they both began to cry. Lauren shut the door, and the three of them collapsed together in the great room under the weight of their fear and anxiety.

3. Life Endures

Ethan was the first to break from their combined grief. He sniffled up his tears and pouted. "I'm hungry, Sissy."

Lauren composed herself and wiped her nose and eyes on her apron. "Breakfast is still on the table. I guess we should eat."

Ethan got up and grabbed Lauren's hand as if he was afraid to lose another connection with the family. She got up, and Aiden pulled a handkerchief out of his pocket, dabbed at his own tears with the corner, then put it over Ethan's nose. "Blow, little buddy."

Ethan blew his nose into the cloth, and Aiden carefully wiped the tears from his little brother's freckled cheeks. Then the three of them took their places at the rough-hewn kitchen table.

Ethan took a bite of his eggs and made a disgusted face, "They're cold and rubbery, Sissy."

"The eggs are just fine." Lauren took a big bite of eggs and then grimaced as she swallowed. "See," she said unconvincingly.

"You don't like them either, Sissy," Ethan shot back.

Lauren's face turned red. "Well, eat your oatmeal then!"

Ethan's spoon was embedded in the oatmeal where he had left it earlier. When he picked it up, the entire bowl of boiled oats came out attached to the spoon. For a brief moment, Ethan sat there with his mouth open as wide as he could get it, then he tried to figure out how to orient the congealed mass to take a bite. Unsuccessful, he whined. "It's bigger than my head."

Aiden let out a deep belly laugh, and a smirk pulled the left side of Lauren's mouth. "Ethan, you are so silly," she said. "But you're right. This isn't very good. Mother wouldn't be happy if we wasted any of it, though. I'll try to rescue it for lunch."

"But I'm hungry now!" Ethan pleaded most pitifully.

Lauren got up from the table and found one of the two loaves of bread Mother had left them with. She cut two thick slices for each of them and put them on a wooden plate. This left just a thick heel from the loaf. Then she put a teaspoon of strawberry jam on each and took the plate to the table.

"We don't have much bread, so enjoy it," Lauren told the boys as they began to devour their bread. They finished their meal in silence, then Lauren pulled the serving spoon out of the empty spider pot and used it to scrape their bowls of oatmeal back into it.

Lauren put her hands flat on the table and looked seriously at the boys. "We can't be wasteful. Mama didn't leave much bread, and we don't know how long she'll be gone. With the summer heat, the chickens aren't laying much, the crops aren't ripe yet, and Clarabelle isn't producing much milk, either."

Then she got a tin cup and tried to fill it from the crock, but it ran dry before the cup filled completely. "I was going to let this soak a little and try to reheat it for lunch, but we're out of water."

"Aiden can get it; he's strong." Ethan offered with pride showing in his eyes.

29

"Aiden has a different job. We let the fire go out." Lauren pointed to the oven. "I thought you could get the water, E."

"But I'm just little; can you do it, Sissy?" Ethan pouted at his sister with puppy-dog eyes.

Lauren shook her head. "You're not too little to bring some water. Maybe you can say hi to Sparkle Frog while you're down there."

Ethan's pouty puppy face turned into a big grin at the thought of seeing Sparkle Frog. "OK, Sissy, I'll try. But if it's too hard, you'll help me, right?"

"It's not going to be too hard. So, move along. The water's not going to fetch itself." Lauren turned to Aiden. "Do you think you can start the fire while I clean up?"

"Sure thing, Sissy," Aiden replied as he got up from the table.

The boys left the cabin and went their separate ways as Lauren worked on cleaning the kitchen. Father had picked an excellent location for their home. A freshwater stream ran nearby. They used it if the well went dry or the windmill malfunctioned, like now. The house's foundation sat on a hill that kept the house from flooding during heavy rains. Father also set the barn and other farm structures only a short walk away.

Ethan didn't see his father's wisdom because he was whining inside about how he had to lug the wooden bucket for miles and miles just to fetch water. Tiredness made him irritable, and he nearly about-faced to tell Lauren he wasn't going. Then sunlight reflected off the dew on the grass and reminded him of Sparkle Frog. Father had said that Sparkle Frog was a very rare type of frog, a Zourian Flying

Rainbow Frog. Ethan knew that Sparkle Frog didn't actually fly, but he had seen him jump at least fifty paces.

Ethan's favorite thing about Sparkle Frog was how the sunlight reflected from his back as he jumped. The frog became a flying rainbow. The thought of seeing Sparkle Frog motivated Ethan, bucket in hand, to run down the hill.

Ethan's enthusiasm was short-lived. He stopped in a shady spot next to the creek where the trees completely blocked the sight of the tower. He set his bucket down and called for his friend, "Sparkle Frog, come out and play!" And he looked over, under, and around the tall grasses and creekside rocks for his friend.

His expectant cries turned to disappointment in not finding his friend. He thought about checking the other side of the creek but was discouraged to see how high the creek water was. The recent storms had filled the creek to its banks, and it was flowing faster than he'd ever seen. He crept up to the side of the stream and stared at the rapidly flowing stream.

Fear gripped Ethan in its icy grasp. The stranger who'd come to their door had said Daddy was washed away by the river. If Daddy couldn't stand up to the flow, how could he? He didn't want to get washed away, but they needed the water. He just couldn't do it; he was too little.

Then there was a flash of light from his right and a familiar "quack." Ethan turned to see Daddy Duck land in a sunlit stretch of water a few paces away. A tree had fallen into the creek, creating a little bay out of the main flow of the water. Ethan walked out of the shade and realized he could get water from there safely.

"Thank you, Daddy Duck. You saved me," Ethan said with relief.

"Quack!" the duck said before diving under the water.

Ethan struggled with the right way to dip water out of the creek at first. The wood bucket floated, so he had to get it at the right angle to get it to fill up. When the bucket was full to the brim, it was too heavy for him to pull out. After multiple tries, he got the bucket three-quarters full and was able to pull it out and carry it.

"I did it!" he exclaimed to Daddy Duck.

The duck looked at him as if to say, "of course you did."

Ethan felt so pleased with himself that he immediately sprinted up the hill despite the bucket weighing him down. When he entered the kitchen, he saw that over half of the water had sloshed out all over his pants and shirt, which dampened his spirits again.

He put the bucket on the counter by the water crock, climbed up next to it, then managed to lift his bucket and pour it into the five-gallon, white-enameled water crock. The quart or so of water barely covered the bottom of it.

Exasperated, Ethan exclaimed, "Not fair! I got the hard job!" as he realized just how many trips it was going to take to bring up the day's water supply.

Just then, Aiden walked back into the kitchen with pieces of split wood for the fire. That looked even heavier than the water bucket.

Not wanting to seem like a baby, Ethan sniffed up his pout, jumped off the counter, and ran back down the hill to get more water, thinking: *If my big brother can get his jobs done, so can I!*

As he ran, he tried to figure out how to get the water crock filled up quickly. Father had always been there to help him figure out how to solve a problem. The more he thought, the more he realized that a big part of his problem was how much water had sloshed out when he ran. This time, he took extra care to fill the bucket and then slowly walked up the hill.

Ethan was able to make four trips without incident. When he got to the kitchen the fifth time, Aiden was carefully blowing at the base of the fire, creating a bigger flame. He turned to Ethan and exclaimed, "I did it! I started the fire!" He pointed at his glowing creation. "Look, E. We're going to have lunch soon!" Then Aiden went to the table and used the handle to carry the spider pot and set it on the floor beside the fireplace. "Sissy will be surprised that we got lunch ready. Since you got the water, do you want to put it in?"

Ethan got so excited at the responsibility of helping in another way he didn't really think about what he was doing and just dumped the entire bucket into the pot. It overflowed, spilling all over the floor. Luckily, the oatmeal was still a congealed blob stuck to the bottom, so little of it washed out.

"I did it too!" Ethan exclaimed.

Aiden looked really mad for an instant—as if Ethan had done something wrong. Then Aiden's expression softened, "You did it too." Aiden shook his head and chuckled.

As the water began to drain between the floorboards, Ethan asked, "When will it be ready?"

"It shouldn't take too long; we just have to get it in the oven," Aiden said as he put the cast iron lid on the spider pot.

Aiden seemed to strain to lift the pot off the floor with the added weight of the water and the lid. "Do you need help?" Ethan asked.

"I've got it," Aiden huffed back. He switched from using the handle to squatting down and wrapping the pot in a bear hug. He was able to get it off the ground, but since the fireplace in the kitchen was a brick oven that was chest-high for Aiden, he had to strain to get the pot in place. He was finally able to rest one of the pot's three feet on the brick edge of the fireplace and then quickly re-oriented his hands to the sides to keep from getting burned.

Just then, Lauren came inside carrying a slab of ham and said excitedly, "I found the last bit of ham!"

This distracted Aiden; as he pushed the pot further into the fireplace, a foot spike caught on a gap in the bricks, and it tipped toward the fire; water cascaded out. Before Aiden could correct his movement, the spider pot tipped further, and the lid slid off, crashing into the flames and scattering the wood inside the fireplace.

The fire hissed and snapped as liquid engulfed it. Before Aiden's eyes, the water extinguished his beautiful fire.

Lauren rushed up to try to help Aiden, ham in hand. Then the whole thing backwashed ashy water and partially burnt sticks out of the fireplace and all down Aiden's shirt.

The floor was already wet from Ethan's spill, and the ashy sludge added to the slippery mess. Lauren's leather-bottomed shoes slid, and she prevented herself from falling

34

by dropping the slab of meat and catching the side of the oven. The ham landed with a plop in the middle of the ashy slime.

At the same time, more smoke and steam than could be handled by the flue billowed out of the oven, cloaking the kitchen into momentary darkness as it obscured the light from the window.

"Aiden!" Ethan yelled. "How are we going to have oaka-meal now? The fire's drownded!" Not only had the fire died, but now he'd have to fetch more water.

"Aiden, what were you thinking!" Lauren blurted out as her whole face went red. Ethan could almost feel the heat radiating off her as she yelled. "That was our last ham! It's ruined."

"I guess I didn't lift it high enough. I couldn't really see. It was really heavy." Aiden turned red, his eyes downcast.

Lauren paused for a moment, taking a deep breath as if she were composing herself. A tiny gust of wind cleared the smoke and steam. Then she said evenly, "Maybe next time, don't fill it so full and let me help you." Lauren put an arm around Aiden's shoulder to give him a hug.

"I'm sorry," Aiden said as he hung his head. "I didn't mean to mess things up. I had a real fire and everything. We were going to do it on our own to surprise you."

Lauren pulled both brothers close. "I appreciate that you wanted to surprise me, but we can't afford to waste a thing right now. I know you want to be strong like Daddy. But he always says sometimes, being strong is knowing when you need to ask for help. Ask for help next time, OK?"

Aiden nodded.

Ethan realized that he was going to have to get more water, and now his stomach was really growling. "I want oaka-meal, and I want it now! I'm hungry, and getting water is hard!" Ethan stomped his foot. "I need food."

"Let's not fight or get grumbly," Lauren said as she squatted down to Ethan's eye level and put her hands on his shoulders. "That's what the Dark One wants."

"OK, Sissy," Ethan replied sheepishly. "But what are we going to eat?"

Lauren looked around the kitchen and shook her head. "It's going to take a while to clean up the mess to be able to make another fire."

"I'm sorry, Sissy," Aiden apologized again.

"It will be alright." Lauren patted him on the shoulder. "I really wanted to keep the bread for the Sabbath as I'm not sure I can make the overnight oatmeal work, but I guess we'll have bread and jam again now and find out about the oatmeal tomorrow."

As Lauren reached for the bread knife, they heard the squishy clip-clop of hoofbeats from out the kitchen window.

Ethan wondered who could be coming to their house. Was Mama coming home? "Sissy! Let's see who it is!" Ethan cried as he rushed out the kitchen door, and Lauren and Aiden hurried to follow.

4. The Visitor

In the distance, Lauren could make out a horse and wagon, and she heard the thud of horse hooves against the damp earth. Might this be the help Mother said the parson would send? Lauren straightened her dress and apron, then stepped back into the house to get a bonnet off the hook by the door. She'd been remiss for not putting it on sooner. Mother was very clear that proper young ladies always wore a bonnet outdoors. Once she had made herself presentable, she stepped onto the porch where the boys were waiting to greet the visitor.

The cart rounded the corner of their house and came into view. Prickles ran up and down Lauren's arms. It was the parson himself!

Ethan turned to Lauren, "Sissy! It's the parson! Maybe he's got food!"

This was the first time she'd taken a good look at Ethan since coming into the house. He was soaked from carrying water. She eyed Aiden and realized he was covered with ashy mud from the fireplace incident. Mother would be mortified for them to meet the parson like this.

"Boys! You are a complete mess! Inside, quick!" Lauren urged the boys toward the door.

"But Sissy!" Ethan whined.

Aiden looked himself over. "C'mon, E. Sissy's right. We look like hog slop right now. We need to change quickly."

She rushed through the kitchen into the great room, where she opened the trunk that held the boys' clothes. She got them each a clean work outfit plus two towels. "Here."

She handed them the towels and clothes. "Dry off and go change. Quick, now. We don't want to keep the parson waiting."

Lauren dashed back into the kitchen and grabbed the round straw broom from beside the fireplace, and used it to push the wet sticks, ruined ham, and ash sludge into a pile. Then she quickly scooped it up and put it in the tin ash bucket.

Lauren looked out the kitchen window as she finished her chore and watched the parson park the wagon in front of their house. She walked out of the house at a deliberate pace in time to see him get down from his seat and wrap the reins around the hitching post attached to their porch.

"Miss Lauren," he said, looking her in the eyes. "It is excellent to see you this fine morning."

"It's nice to see you as well, parson," Lauren replied and gave a simple curtsey.

The parson stepped onto the porch, took off his circular-brimmed straw hat, and then dabbed at his forehead with a bleached handkerchief. The way he carefully folded the cloth and put it back reminded Lauren how dignified she thought he was, despite his thinning silver hair and the plain-white linen smock and trousers he wore.

"I came as soon as the missus would let me go. I hope you children haven't had any troubles this morning," the parson said as he put his hat back on.

"No, sir, not really," Lauren said, her face downcast as she fretted about the disaster lunch had become. Mother had put her in charge, and so far, they could barely feed themselves. What would the parson think of her?

"Did Mrs. Miller come by yet to watch over you?" The parson looked about the yard and peered toward the barn. "I don't see their horse and buggy."

Lauren's eyebrows rose. "No, sir, she didn't."

"How about Mr. Carpenter? He was to come by this morning and help to feed and water the animals."

"No, sir." Lauren shook her head, "No one has been by today."

"Well, that is curious. Very curious indeed. I sent the bishop's acolyte off with specific instructions to pass on to both families. He claimed to have a fast horse." The parson sighed. "Well, there's nothing to do about that right now." He stepped off the porch and got a picnic basket out of his wagon. "I guess that means there's more of the missus's fried chicken and rhubarb pie for you children, then. Does that sound good?"

"Oh, yes, sir, it does." Lauren nearly forgot about her worries, knowing that her stomach would soon be full despite the disaster of this morning's adventure in cooking.

The parson handed her the basket, which reminded Lauren of all the times Mother prepared delicious food in baskets like this for other families. She stood up straight. She'd nearly forgotten her manners!

"Sir, we'd be honored if you would eat with us."

The parson smiled. "I can't pass up my wife's cooking."

Lauren smiled back. It felt good to have an adult here, someone more experienced with facing problems caused by the Darkness. "I'll need to get the boys," she told the parson. "Please follow me, and we'll get you settled." Lauren motioned toward the kitchen door.

"Very well. I'll water my horse first." The parson reached for the spigot next to the water trough in front of the house.

"The windmill was broken the other night in the storm." Lauren pointed to the blades still embedded in the ground halfway between the house and the barn. "We weren't expecting you, so we didn't fill the trough this morning. I'll get some water from the kitchen."

"You show me where the water is, and I'll take care of it." The parson stepped back onto the porch and followed Lauren inside. She got a bucket and put it under the spigot of the water crock, and started filling it.

"I can get the food ready to eat," Lauren said with a little more force than she meant to. She was starving, and she could pick up the faint smell of fried chicken from within the basket.

The parson handed her the basket and turned to watch the bucket fill up. "You go right ahead. This will just be a minute."

Lauren went to the kitchen table and began to lay out the fried chicken and pie. She was amazed by the feast in the basket. There were also mashed potatoes, gravy, and rolls. As she put out the mashed potatoes, she caught herself trying to swipe a finger full out of the bowl like when she was little. She looked over her shoulder and saw the parson was carrying the bucket out to his horse.

Lauren began to set the table with fragile, white-enameled ceramic plates and the real silverware that Mother only got out for guests. When the parson came back in, Lauren asked, "Parson, will water be OK? We don't have a fire for coffee or tea, but I think Aiden could get that going."

"Water would be just fine, child. May I help?"

"No, sir. This meal is enough." Her heart swelling with gratitude, Lauren filled four tin cups with water from the crock.

The boys burst into the kitchen. The buttons on Ethan's shirt were off by one, and Aiden only had half of his shirt tucked in. "Pie!" they said in unison as they saw the feast on the table. Licking their lips, they popped into their seats.

Lauren set down the tin cups and took her seat. The parson said grace, and immediately the boys grabbed for fried chicken. Lauren was about to correct them, but the parson said, "You mentioned that the storm blew off the windmill blades."

Lauren saw that the parson wasn't going to correct them on manners today, so she relaxed and served herself mashed potatoes while Aiden explained, "It wasn't the wind. It was lightning." Aiden paused and seemed to be waiting to make sure the parson was paying attention. "The Dark One did it."

"Are you sure?" asked the parson.

"Definitely." Aiden washed down bites of chicken with water. "The shaft looks melted, like metal in a forge. Only lightning can do that."

"Aiden thinks it was the Dark One 'cause he says Daddy put the lightning rods up, and the lightning hit where it wasn't supposed to." Ethan's chin lifted as he showed pride in his brother. Ethan fisted his right hand and shook it toward the window. "I'm gonna conk the Dark

One in his wonkus for making us carry all that water and for taking my Daddy away."

Lauren's lips tightened. "Ethan, I don't think you'll be going after the Dark One anytime soon."

"In the Good Book, a little boy, who had God on his side, beat a giant that scared a whole army," Ethan declared. "If God wants us to go save Daddy, we will."

"Young Ethan, you are exactly right. The Good Book is full of examples where the Spirit of the Lord helps an unlikely person defeat evil." The parson pointed toward the great room, where Father's copy of the Good Book was visible. "If you read carefully, you will discover more miracles like this in its pages. You will see them in your own life only if the Lord calls you to them." He clasped his hands together. "So, young Ethan, I hope you ask God to go with you before you go conking any wonkuses, OK?"

"Yes, sir," Ethan said as he looked down at his plate with a pout on his lips.

Lauren had her doubts but kept them to herself. She believed the Good Book and knew that God worked through people, but if He was so powerful, why had He let her mother and father disappear?

The parson turned to face the children. "Your parents will be very proud of your insight and to hear how hard you've worked. I know how hard it must have been to get water from the creek when you are used to running water."

The children nodded and sighed. It felt so good to be encouraged.

"When your father put in a windmill for us, it was such a blessing. I don't know why other Heathlands families didn't take advantage of his skill."

"Do you know how it works?" asked Aiden.

The parson shook his head. "Not exactly. Why do you ask?"

"If I knew how it worked, I could make it pump by hand somehow until Daddy gets back." Aiden scooped up some mashed potatoes as he began to imagine ways he might be able to fix it.

The parson smiled. "I'm not mechanical, and with my old bones, I won't be any help in climbing up to fix anything. However, I can show you how your father primed mine when you are done eating."

Aiden began wolfing down his food with abandon. He knew deep down he could figure out how to pump the water if he could just get a good look at it.

"Pie, Aiden?" Lauren asked as Aiden put the leg bone he'd just eaten clean on his otherwise empty plate.

Aiden jumped up from the table. "We can save dessert for later. Let's go!"

Ethan interjected, "Aiden, I want pie now!"

Lauren rolled her eyes. "Ethan, how about we let Aiden figure this out, and then we'll come back for pie."

"If he fixes it, do I have to carry buckets anymore?" Ethan asked earnestly.

"No, the water will come to the house like before," Aiden replied as he hopped out of his chair.

"OK, we can save the pie for later." Ethan got up from the table with Lauren right behind him.

The parson wiped his hands on a napkin and followed them.

At the base of the windmill, the parson pointed to a ladder on the side of the tall structure. "See that?" he asked.

43

Aiden shaded his eyes with his hand. "Yes, sir."

"It leads up to a reservoir," the parson continued. "At my place, your father climbed up the outside of the windmill and had me hand him a bucket of water. He poured water into the top of the pump, then jiggled that arm until water poured from the pump into the top of the reservoir."

Scratching his head, Aiden studied the mechanism. "I can't climb up the windmill like that. Daddy's a lot taller than me. Even if I could get up there on a ladder or something, I don't think I could reach the arm."

The arm was at least twice as high as he was tall. Aiden remembered something he'd seen that just might work.

"Be right back." Aiden dashed off to the barn, then returned with a wooden-handled garden rake. With both hands, he held it up above his head and used it to push up on the arm until he met resistance and couldn't lift it any higher. Then he flipped the rake so the hooked end was on top of the handle and pulled it down.

"Aiden!" cried Ethan, who had joined them. "I saw water come out! You fixed it!"

Aiden pumped several times, alternating the position of the rake. It was awkward and slow. Finally, he said, "This is too hard. Hold on."

He zipped to the barn and returned with a garden harrow. It had a long handle like the rake, but on one end had three curved hooks at the top, offset by two curved hooks four inches lower.

Aiden lifted the harrow, hooked the top hooks over the bar, and pulled down. Then he pushed up, and the two lower hooks caught on the bar.

44

"Master Aiden," the parson beamed, "that is a fantastic bit of barnyard ingenuity. You really are your father's son."

Thank you, sir," Aiden said, his cheeks red from embarrassment.

The parson moved so he could look at all the children as he talked. "You children have things very much in hand. Your parents have taught you well."

"Thank you, Parson. We've done our best, but there's much that we can't do." Lauren pleaded with the parson.

"I am shocked that the other families I asked to help have not come." The parson got down on one knee and motioned the children closer. "I will look into this personally and get you some help this evening. I shouldn't have trusted that boy from far off to deliver the message." The parson shook his head. Aiden wondered who this stranger was and why he wouldn't help them.

"I have a meeting with the bishop this afternoon and will definitely let him know his acolyte was remiss in his duties. God willing, I'll return myself to make sure you children are properly looked after."

Aiden nodded, sharing the parson's concerns. "Mama said she would only be gone a couple of days."

"God willing, she will be here soon with your father in tow." The parson stood back up.

"Amen," Ethan declared to Aiden's surprise.

"Amen indeed. If I don't see you this evening, then be sure to find me tomorrow at services." The parson turned and walked toward his horse.

The children followed him to the porch and waited as he untied the reins of his horse and got into the buggy. "I'll be seeing you soon." The parson waved to the children.

The children returned to the kitchen, which seemed dark and dull now that the parson had left. Aiden remembered that Father had always said that so long as they were obedient in the little things, their light would shine brightly. Somehow, though their spirits were down, they would manage to do the little things with a happy heart. The Light to show Mother and Father their way home depended on it.

5. The Discovery

Neither the parson nor any of the families he'd mentioned had come to help them that day. This worried Lauren greatly and had her on edge. As evening came, she asked the boys to get a fire going in the kitchen stove and to reheat the leftovers from the feast the parson had brought for them.

After dinner and clean-up, Lauren pulled out the slate, determined to keep a regular bedtime routine. "Ethan, let's practice your letters to keep your hands busy while Aiden reads the Good Book. Mother will be so proud."

Ethan nodded. "I will work really hard." He grabbed the slate and got to work.

Then Lauren sent Aiden for the Good Book and encouraged him to read aloud.

"Hey!" Ethan stopped his slate work. "Find the story about the boy and the giant!"

Lauren knew there was no changing Ethan's mind, so she found the chapter. As Aiden read, Ethan added commentary. "See, he was the littlest in his family, and his family wasn't even that important." He was so excited his knee jarred the slate. "His brothers, the king, even the whole army trembled with fear at that giant's taunts. Not the boy!" Ethan puffed out his chest. "The boy knew God would help him."

After Aiden had read for a while, Ethan interrupted, "Wait!" He waved his arms. "See? God gave him the power to conk the giant on the wonkus! Sissy, if God helped that little boy, He can help us."

As Aiden finished the story, Lauren just nodded. She did believe God watched over them and that even in their trouble, God had a plan. It was just hard to understand or know what might happen next. In a way, she wished she could feel as sure as Ethan did. Lauren yawned, tired from her doubts, tired from the day's work. Though it was early, she'd send the boys to bed. Even with the help the parson promised, they would likely still have much to do tomorrow just to eat breakfast.

"It's too early," Aiden protested. "I gotta stoke the fire, and hey, what do you think is in that bag?" He pointed at the sack the Mighty Mercenary had left behind the coat tree.

The end of a wooden staff or a spear poked out of the top of the bag, the mouth of the sack tied tightly around it. The rod had a rounded steel cap on the end that extended about four inches down the shaft. Aiden walked over and tried to pick up the sack, but it wouldn't budge. He knocked it on its side and tried to drag it, but it still didn't go anywhere.

"Lauren, would you help?" he cried, but no matter how they pushed, pulled, or prodded the sack, it wouldn't move. They even asked Ethan to help. Finally, Aiden said, "This must hold Daddy's armor or something really heavy. Let's open it and see what's weighing it down."

The children pushed the sack upright and untied it. As they pulled the bag open, it fell over in a heap. On top was a shield so huge it would hide all three of them. It was so shiny and smooth that it acted like a mirror. A relief in the image of the lantern in the Tower of Light was stamped in the center.

The metal-ended wooden rod and the pommel of Father's sword both protruded from under the shield's edge. The shield covered so much space they couldn't tell if anything else was in the bag.

Aiden reached for the part of the shield that stuck out of the bag and tried to move it, but no matter how he strained, it seemed glued to the floor. Lauren helped, to no avail. She wondered if the bag would have to sit in the great room until Mother and Father got home.

"I can help," Ethan exclaimed and reached for the handle of Father's sword. Much like with the shield, the sword wouldn't move, no matter how hard he tried. Lauren tried the sword as well and couldn't even push it aside.

Aiden ran his hand through his hair, then exclaimed, "I've got it! We'll use the wooden rod like a lever to pry the rest of it loose."

It was a great idea, but it failed, just as Ethan's attempt had. As Aiden let go of the rod, Ethan tried to grab it to help, but he tripped over the sword's hilt and caught his balance on the side of the shield.

"I feel tingly!" Ethan exclaimed as he wrapped his fingers more tightly around the edge of the shield. It began to shrink, "Sissy, looky!" The shield continued to shrink until it was the size of a small buckler that fit Ethan perfectly. "It's just my size!"

The shield's surface reflected the light in the room, forcing the children to squint and take a minute to refocus their eyes.

"Wow!" they all exclaimed.

Ethan put the shield on his arm. "Look, Aiden. I'm just like Daddy!"

"I don't understand." Lauren was dumbfounded by what she'd just seen. "We couldn't even move it. When Ethan touches it, pop, it's small and light, perfect for him."

"Hey, E," Aiden demanded. "Let me try." He reached for the shield.

"Do I have to?" Ethan whined to Lauren as if hoping she'd say no.

Lauren paused for a moment, unsure what was going on, but not sharing wouldn't be good. "He'll give it right back, E."

Ethan handed the shield to Aiden reluctantly. As soon as the shield left his hand, it reshaped back to full size and threatened to crush Aiden. Ethan grabbed it, and immediately the shield returned to "Ethan size."

"That is amazing!" Aiden exclaimed.

Lauren couldn't believe he completely ignored the fact that he was almost crushed.

Aiden reached into the heap. "What else is in this bag?" He put his hand on the rod with the metal ends. Though he grunted with effort, he couldn't pick it up. "E, you try!"

Ethan pulled and pushed, to no avail, which confused all three children. If Ethan had the power to pick up the shield, why couldn't he do the same with this rod?

"E, why don't you try the sword? Maybe it goes with the shield," Aiden said.

Ethan pulled and groaned with no effect on the large weapon.

Finally, Lauren said, "Let me try." She reached for the rod, and as her fingers wrapped around it, she felt a sensation like warm water running over her arms. The weapon handle was reduced in width to fit her hand more comfortably. Then one end formed a spear tip made of an aquamarine glow around the metal tip. Indeed, the whole spear glowed with a light that flowed like water. As Lauren gripped the weapon with both hands, the radiance ran over her fingers, as did the watery aura.

"Whoa!" Aiden took a step back from Lauren. "That's amazing."

"Aiden, I'll bet that's for you." Lauren set the base of the spear on the floor and pointed to the sword with her other hand. "I never touched that, and it didn't move when E tripped over it. I'll bet it's yours."

Aiden reached for the sword hilt. The instant he touched it, he said, "I feel a fire in my chest." The sword shrank from a two-handed longsword for a grown-up to the size of a short sword that Aiden could wield in a two-handed grip.

A blue-white flame burst out along the sword handle, startling Aiden, who dropped it. The fire disappeared, and the sword returned to its full size as it clattered to the floor.

"Oops," he said, red-faced. Then he picked it up more carefully, and the fire returned. He could feel the heat from the flame, but it didn't hurt him.

"Aiden, that is awesome." Envy shrilled Ethan's voice. "I like yours better."

To distract Ethan, Lauren asked, "Boys, did you feel something when you touched your weapons for the first time?"

"Yeah, Sissy." Ethan fitted the shield on his arm with its straps. "It made me all tingly up and down my back."

Aiden swiped the air hesitantly with the sword. "I feel a fire in my heart."

51

"I feel a warm wave as if I put my hand in bathwater."
With both hands, Lauren gripped the middle of the spear,
watching the light flow over her hands. "If I set it down,
will the glow stop?"

To test her theory, Lauren bent to lay the spear on the
ground. As soon as she let go, the shaft remained the same
shape, but the glow receded, and the warm feeling
disappeared. Lauren picked it back up, and the spear shaft
remained perfectly sized to her hand, but the blue-green
spear tip and flowing energy did not return. "Oh!" she
cried. "Boys put yours down." They complied, and the fire
left the sword, and the glow on the shield diminished, but
their shapes were retained. When the children picked them
back up, the light and the fire didn't return.

"The tingle's gone!" Ethan exclaimed. "That's not fair!
What about your fire, Aiden?"

Aiden's face fell. Finally, he said, "I don't feel it
anymore."

Lauren saw the disappointment on their faces. "Boys, I
think it's probably OK. Daddy made these weapons, and
now we can carry them. I have a feeling that if we need the
power they have, it will come to us."

"You mean like the boy who fought the giant?" Ethan
asked excitedly.

Lauren set the staff against the wall and began sorting
through the clothes, pouches, and pieces of armor still in
the pile. "I've read lots of stories in the Good Book where
things like this happen. Ethan might be right about God
using little people to do big jobs, like the boy who fought
the giant."

"Do you think God has a plan for us that includes these weapons?" Aiden asked as he inspected his sword, tracing the inscription along the handguard with his fingers.

Lauren stacked the gear up as she set to organizing with Ethan's help. "I don't know, Aiden. We need to talk to the parson tomorrow at church. He might know what to do."

Ethan picked up his shield and put it back on. "OK, Sissy, but I'm taking this to bed to keep the monsters and dragons in my dreams away."

"All right," Lauren said. "But first, we'll finish cleaning up."

They tidied up the house, climbed up to the loft, and got ready for bed.

"Sissy, Pray!" Ethan said as she tucked him into bed.

Lauren folded her hands together and bowed her head, "God bless, Mama. God bless Daddy. God, keep the monsters, dragons, and Dark One away. Amen."

"Amen," said the boys in unison.

Lauren climbed into her own bed and contemplated the day's events. Now that they were armed for battle against the Darkness. What would God do next?

6. A Stranger at Church

Lauren awoke with a start. Despite the passion in her prayer the night before, she'd had a terrifying dream. She'd been surrounded by darkness and could sense someone near her was chained in place by unseen bonds. As she rose from her bed, the boys must have detected her movements because they both whined.

"Sissy, do we have to get up?" Aiden rolled over and pulled the blanket over his head.

"No." Lauren patted him. "You can sleep a while longer. I just had a bad dream and can't go back to sleep."

Aiden sat up straight. "Was it about being trapped in darkness?"

Lauren took a step back. "Yes, only it wasn't me who was trapped. It was someone else."

Ethan's sheets rustled as he also sat up. His face grim and ashy, he said, "It was Mama, and I saw her tied up in the dark." Ethan acted like he was holding an imaginary lamp. "I shined my light on the person, then saw Mama's face. I tried to shine a way out for her, but Sissy woke me up."

"What light, Ethan?" She didn't understand. They'd all had the same dream. But why did Ethan have a light to shine while she and Aiden did not? "Ethan, what light did you shine?"

"My shield. I held up my shield, and it shined the Light on Mama," Ethan said and held up his shield.

Lauren remembered that he had taken the shield to bed. Her staff was leaning against the wall, next to Aiden's sword. If they had all taken their arms to bed, would they have been able to free Mother? Did the dream mean that Mother had been taken by the Darkness too? What about Father? So many questions and no real answers. She felt so frustrated and confused.

"I don't know what's going on here," Lauren said, "but I know we need some help to understand. We need to hurry to church so we can talk to the parson."

With that, Lauren rushed down the ladder and got a pot ready with rolled oats for lunch later that day. The boys followed Lauren after a couple of minutes, and Aiden set to stoking the coals into flame.

Lauren sent the boys out to do the bare minimum chores to take care of the animals. She always liked the civility of the Sabbath. The beautiful clothes made the day special and somehow sophisticated. Even the way they took care of their Sabbath clothes was very particular. She went to her parent's room and took her simple white ankle-length dress from the cedar chest, and put it on. After squeezing into her knee-length, brown leather boots, she smoothed the skirt of her dress. She took good care of them, regularly oiling and putting shapers in them if they got wet, but she had grown so much this last year that they were almost too tight.

When she was ready, she returned to the kitchen and put on her apron. The flames had died down enough that she could put on the spider pot. As she finished putting coals on top of it, the boys came in.

Lauren knew the boys didn't share her love for the Sabbath because they had to wear shoes. Living on the farm, they preferred the feeling of grass and mud between their toes. "Boys, get ready for church. Before you ask, yes, you have to wear shoes." The boys rolled their eyes at her. "We'll have some bread and then go so we can get there early, OK?"

"OK, Sissy," they huffed in unison.

Lauren cut bread and put jelly on it like the day before. This was the last of it, but hopefully, someone at church would be able to help them get more supplies.

As Lauren hoped, the boys came back into the kitchen, both wearing khaki cotton pants, white short-sleeved linen shirts, and brown leather shoes that squeaked on the wooden floor. What she didn't expect was that they were also armed.

"Boys, what are you doing?" Lauren demanded.

"Going to church," Aiden replied with a raised eyebrow.

"I mean, why are you carrying a sword?" Lauren pointed at his weapon.

"If we're going to talk to the parson about it, doesn't it make sense to show him?" Aiden replied matter-of-factly.

"Oh!" Lauren replied, taken aback by the simple logic of Aiden's response.

Ethan added enthusiastically, "Yeah, Sissy, my shield shined the Light for Mama. I want to show the parson."

"Whoa, hold on." Lauren put up her hands, "I know that makes a certain amount of sense. But I don't think people will understand if a bunch of kids show up armed for battle. I'm sure the parson will come home with us to inspect them if he needs to."

Aiden looked thoughtful. "You're probably right, Sissy. E, we can show him later."

"OK." Ethan pointed at Lauren. "I'm going to be really mad if we run into the Dark One, and I don't have my shield."

That issue resolved, the children began the two-mile walk to the chapel. After reaching the main road, they crossed a little bridge over the creek. Sparkle Frog was in the creek on the church side of the bridge and leapt onto the bridge railing. There was no rainbow.

"Sissy! Did you see that?" Ethan exclaimed. "Sparkle Frog didn't sparkle."

Lauren was taken aback by this. The Frog was always literally a bright point in her day. As she looked at the end of the bridge, she could vaguely make out an odd haze. It wasn't fog or clouds, but the light ahead of them was dimmer. It was seven o'clock, and the sun had been up and shining for an hour, yet the other side of the bridge had taken on an early twilight hue.

Fear gripped Lauren, and she began to turn back to go home, but then she thought of Mother going off to save Father. Squeezing her hands into fists to steel her resolve, she said, "Something is very wrong, boys. We need to get to the parson and get to the bottom of this. C'mon."

"What about Sparkle Frog?" Ethan asked as he reached for his frog.

"Oh, no, you don't." Lauren grabbed Ethan's hand and motioned for Aiden to come along. "You two cause trouble when you're together. Sparkle Frog can stay here by the creek. He should be safe enough till we come back."

Ethan's lips were pursed, and his eyebrows were scrunched up like he was about to protest, but Aiden said, "E, Sissy's right. Let's hurry and ask the parson."

"OK." Ethan relented and took off ahead at top speed. Aiden jogged after, and Lauren followed. She looked over her shoulder to see Sparkle Frog lazily hopping after them. She hoped she was right about the frog not being in any real danger.

Ethan quickly slowed and turned back to look at Lauren." Why is it brighter behind us?"

Lauren felt that the closer they got to the church, the darker everything seemed. "I don't know. We can ask the parson, but we need to hurry." Lauren was focused on getting to the church, so much so that she walked right past the boys as they slowed. Her stride quickly outpaced the boys, who had taken to a normal walk after their brief sprint.

Suddenly, Lauren heard a ruckus and whirled about. The boys were trying to shove each other off the road. "Boys!" Lauren hissed, trying not to draw attention to their bad behavior in case anybody was watching.

"He pushed me first," Ethan whined.

"He stepped on my toe," Aiden retorted, a scowl on his face.

"It was an accident, Aiden," Ethan snapped back.

"Enough!" Lauren blurted out, louder than she meant. "Daddy would be very disappointed in you boys acting like this on the way to church."

Suddenly there was a flash of light behind her, and she heard a whoosh of wings and a familiar "quack."

The haze around the boys vanished for a second, and they both stopped in their tracks. Aiden looked at Ethan's dumbfounded expression and said, "We're sorry, Sissy. We'll be good."

Ethan looked down at his feet as he shuffled back and forth. "I'll be good, too."

Daddy Duck landed next to Lauren, cocked his head to one side, and let out a very satisfied "quack." Lauren had seen Daddy Duck flash before, but until now, she'd never paid much attention to Aiden's friend. It seemed like he had flashed away the haze around them. This was something else she would have to ask the parson about.

Lauren started to walk forward, then whirled and got close to the boys. She pulled them to her and whispered, "Something's not right. I don't like this haze. We need to be careful. No more fooling around."

The boys' cheeks were red with embarrassment from their earlier antics, so they just nodded. Lauren continued, "We're going to play the quiet game the rest of the way to church. If you behave, I'll get out the honey for our oatmeal tonight." Since the family didn't keep bees, Lauren knew honey was a rare treat that might entice the boys to follow her direction.

The boys pinched their right index finger to their thumb, ran them across their lips, twisted them to the right, and then threw imaginary keys over their shoulders.

Lauren smiled at this and did the same. She reached down and patted the duck on his head, then motioned for the boys to follow and set off as fast as she could without leaving the boys behind. Both their animal friends followed along as they continued to the church. All the way there, Lauren had the feeling the dark haze was closing in around her.

*** *** ***

When the children stepped inside the church, a strange, cold dread descended on Lauren. In the pews sat only half of those who regularly attended. Absent were the Millers and Carpenters—the families the parson suggested would stop by to help. Lauren shivered. Why would the most devoted families miss service? They came even in the middle of winter when they had to plow a path to the main road.

As the children quietly found places on the back bench, a stranger entered the chapel. Hunched over, he wore a ratty brown cloak. Wisps of oily salt-and-pepper hair did not hide a balding head, and his long, stringy, black beard, as ratty as his cloak, had streaks of gray. He leaned forward as he walked, holding onto what might have been a walking stick, but it looked more like a fighting staff. It had rounded steel ends like Lauren's spear. The man mumbled to himself like someone not right in the head. He sat down on a bench in the middle of the church.

Aiden wrinkled his nose at the sight of this man and opened his mouth to say something.

Lauren squeezed his hand, shook her head, and whispered, "Quiet game."

Both boys nodded and folded their hands in their laps.

As usual, the service opened with a hymn, yet someone new led the congregation. Unlike the parson, who wore the same plain, white clothes as his congregants, save the tiny golden cross pin at his heart for adornment, this man dressed in a dark red, floor-length robe that made him look both regal and official. The thick gold necklace roped around his neck also made him look different from the rest of the congregation.

A large cross encrusted with glittering jewels dangled from the necklace. Even without such fancy attire, he was dazzlingly handsome, with tightly cropped and perfectly groomed jet-black hair. Despite the heavy robe, he appeared to be a powerful and muscular man. The children exchanged puzzled looks but sang along as they always did.

After the hymn, the strange leader introduced himself as the bishop of the region. "The parson has taken … a leave of absence. I will be your spiritual leader for the next few weeks while we find someone to take his place."

Standing to the left and to the right of the bishop stood two teenage boys in similar robes; only theirs were yellow and purple, respectively. As the service went on, these two young men performed the duties of acolytes, attending to the sacraments in a ritualistic manner as the bishop directed them.

Lauren drummed her fingers against the pew, remembering when Mother told her that their parson didn't follow all the traditional rituals because some might drown out the message. Mother liked that about the parson. Now Lauren could see why. Her stomach tightened. This formal style was all so very complicated and foreign to their usual way of worship.

Ethan whispered in Lauren's ear, "Sissy, I've got to go to the outhouse."

"OK, but go quietly," Lauren whispered back as she put a finger to her mouth to emphasize being quiet.

After the opening parts of the service, the bishop began an inspiring message on tolerance. "In Loggerton," his voice rose melodically, "people reduced strife in their community by accepting one another." He raised his arms.

61

"Now, that," he proclaimed, banging his fist on the pulpit for emphasis, "is the primary message of the Good Book: tolerance of all."

Lauren studied him carefully, unsure about his message, but the bishop spoke with such convincing words. He must be speaking the truth. Hadn't her parents taught them to respect their elders? Still, the message didn't hold her attention like the parson's always did. Restless, her mind wandered as she looked around the room.

As the sermon continued, the man in tattered clothes kept shaking his head, almost in sync with the bishop's words. He muttered to himself as he had earlier. Only now, he seemed to do so each time the bishop completed a sermon point.

Lauren rubbed her forehead. Maybe the crazy-looking man wasn't actually crazy.

Ethan came back in, walking backward. Lauren nearly asked, "what on earth are you doing?" but she didn't want to be disruptive. She tried to catch Ethan's attention, but he sat down at the end of the bench, with his back to her as much as he could manage, and he stared at the floor.

The bishop appeared to be drawing to a close in the seemingly never-ending sermon when the tattered old man leapt to his feet. His cloak flowed back behind him as he stood, revealing that he wore the armor of a knight protector.

His breast and shoulder plates were pitted and dented from what looked like a thousand blows, giving them an ancient look. The old man's right shoulder plate was emblazoned with the symbol of Father's cadre. Lauren's heart leapt at the thought of being able to ask him about Father. Maybe he had news about Mother as well.

The old man slammed his staff on the ground three times and yelled at the bishop, "Heretic! This message you spew, 'tolerate others' beliefs, no matter how they behave or what they do,' is not the message of the Good Book!"

Lauren's limbs stiffened. What on earth had just happened? Never in the middle of a sermon had someone stood to disagree about what was or was not in the Good Book. Who was telling the truth, this finely dressed bishop or this raggedy old man, seemingly a knight protector?

The old man stepped toward the front of the church and turned to look at the congregation. "Have you been to Loggerton?" He punctuated each word with a pound of his staff against the floor. The *thud*, *thud* echoed in Lauren's ears, making her wince. "Have you seen how the Darkness has gripped that community?"

Silence reigned in the chapel. Lauren could not take her eyes off the old man. Something deep inside her confirmed his words, his tone, his anger. Plus, he wore the colors of Father's cadre. Her throat tightened. If only Father were here to confirm who spoke the truth.

The battered knight protector threw his arms in the air and raised his face as if toward the heavens. "The Good Book's message is to love God with all your heart and then love others! You cannot love God and tolerate evil!" He pointed at the bishop with his staff. "You preach lies!" With a final slam of his staff against the floor, he hobbled back down the aisle toward the exit, coming close to where the children sat.

As the old knight protector passed them, a smile transformed his strange countenance, erasing his scary look. It was as though he knew them as old family friends. Before he walked past them, his stern look returned, and he continued toward the door.

In the meantime, the two acolytes ducked their heads and looked wide-eyed at the bishop as if wondering what he would do.

The bishop nodded slightly, at which time the acolytes leapt over the prayer rail separating the bishop from the parishioners. They flew down the center aisle toward the old man, who had just cleared the inner doors to the sanctuary. Lauren couldn't see what was happening, but she heard the doors slam shut, then two loud thuds.

Lauren craned her neck to see behind her. Had the acolytes banged into the doors? She glanced at Ethan and Aiden, who must've seen what had happened as they were sitting with their knees on the bench, smiling and nodding.

The acolytes had, in fact, slammed into the doors, and now both sat on the floor by the inner sanctuary doors right behind the end of the kid's bench. The one who wore the yellow robe had blood streaming out of his nose; the other rubbed his forehead, which looked to be bruised.

Now Lauren turned to better see the result of the spectacle that had unfolded behind her. Had the old knight protector slammed the sanctuary doors on the two boys?

Something croaked.

Lauren jumped.

It was Sparkle Frog announcing his presence on Ethan's lap. He then made a leap and hopped onto the head of the purple-robed acolyte, who held his head in his palms, rubbing his temples with his fingers.

Lauren blinked; then, her eyes opened wide. When Sparkle Frog jumped off the acolyte's forehead, the red-looking bump had disappeared. He landed on the boy's shoulder and began to preen himself with an air of satisfaction.

Lauren was always amazed at Sparkle Frog's healing power. Despite this, her face blazed with embarrassment. She had told the boys to behave, and now Ethan had done this! She sat up and tried to appear calm, though she was mortified. What would this high-and-mighty new bishop think about children who brought animals to the service? The parson would have shown them grace, but did this bishop really mean what he said about tolerance?

7.   What is Truth?

The sight of the two official-looking acolytes sitting on the floor in all of their pomp and circumstance, with Sparkle Frog croaking on the boy's shoulder, was just too much for Aiden and Ethan to continue the quiet game.

They looked at each other and broke out into hysterical laughter. Lauren was about to shush them, but something about Sparkle Frog's proud expression was too much for her as well. Giggles escaped from her mouth, despite the mean glares coming from the stunned boys. Others throughout the church began to snicker.

The purple-robed acolyte, with Sparkle Frog on his shoulder, swatted at the frog, hollering, "You stupid frog, get off!"

Sparkle Frog leapt across the room and hopped out of an open window, a rainbow trailing behind him. The sight of the rainbow sent a hush, then murmurs through the church, as if other people also realized the boy's swelling was gone.

Lauren's breath caught. She glanced toward the bishop. What would he do now that everyone was involved in this chaotic scene?

The regal man continued to stand tall, his face not showing any emotion.

Lauren glanced at the boys, embarrassed for herself, embarrassed for her brothers. She'd have to apologize, she guessed, but that didn't seem to settle her conscience. Oh, what was going on?

The bishop cleared his throat and smoothed out the satin-like material of his robe. A smile played with his lips.

Lauren's mouth fell open. The bishop accepted, even agreed with, their humor. How could that be?

Others sitting around her smiled; Lauren couldn't tell if it was from relief that the bishop wasn't mad or if they genuinely found the incident funny.

The bishop continued smiling, then chuckled. His handsome face showed the hint of crow's feet at the corners of his eyes. He stepped down from his lofty position at the front of the chapel.

The crowd again took on a hushed silence as the bishop walked to the end of the aisle, where the acolytes were sprawled, and knelt next to them. He pulled a blood-red handkerchief from an inner pocket and handed it to the yellow-robed boy with the nose injury. The boy took it, wiped his face, then pinched the bridge of his nose and tilted his head back. Then the bishop helped both acolytes to their feet.

"My good people," the bishop began, his voice as silky as his robe, "that old, misguided man's display is precisely the kind of intolerance that encourages the Darkness to spread across our land."

The bishop put his arms around the shoulders of the two boys and walked them to the front of the church. "These young men were merely rushing to the aid of a confused, possibly drunken, old man, who appeared to be unsteady on his feet. How did he respond to their aid? By slamming a door in their faces."

At the front of the church, the boys again at his side, the bishop turned to face the congregation. "Can you imagine any man in his right mind doing such a thing to these servants of God? It is a somber day when even our vaunted knight protectors no longer see the difference between good and evil."

The bishop took his hands off the boys' shoulders and pointed at the window Sparkle Frog had used to escape. "Even God's lesser creatures understand and leap to assist the wronged. Is not the miracle we witnessed here of this young man's wound being healed evidence of our righteousness? This was clearly a brutal attack by an unholy man."

The bishop pointed to Ethan. "God himself must have prompted young Ethan to prepare for such a thing, as I know no proper child would think to bring a frog to services."

Upon hearing his name called, Ethan scooted closer to Lauren and tried to hide behind her. She was shocked that this stranger knew who her brother was.

"Thank you, my son," the bishop continued, "for heeding the Lord's promptings."

Murmurs of agreement broke out in the congregation.

While people nodded and smiled, the bishop motioned for the acolytes to reopen the sanctuary doors. "Let us close with the benediction." The bishop opened a book on the dais and began to read a long formal prayer.

Lauren had a hard time staying mad at Ethan since things had worked out with Sparkle Frog, yet she still felt uneasy. How had Ethan managed to sneak Sparkle Frog into the service? She'd been so concerned about the feeling of the Darkness closing in as they'd come to church that she'd lost track of Sparkle Frog. Ethan must've found the frog near the outhouse and decided to bring him inside.

Had Sparkle Frog been used by God, as the bishop said, or had it been an act of another force? She had seen Sparkle Frog fix bumps and bruises many times. Father said that was how Sparkle Frog was touched by the Light. Lauren remembered the story of the boy defeating the giant. She knew God could use anything. But was a frog sneaking into the church really God's plan? If the Knight hadn't disagreed with the bishop, she would say, of course. But something about all this didn't sit well with her.

As Lauren grappled with her thoughts, the bishop continued the overly formal benediction. Lauren opened her eyes and tapped each of the boys on the shoulder to signal for them to quietly step out of the service. This entire service had been so confusing.

She really had needed the parson to be at church to talk over the meaning of the weapons and the dreams. He was there when they lit the tower, so she knew he understood about the Light and the Darkness. The problem was that the parson was not here.

On the other hand, the bishop was there. He had the authority to give spiritual advice. He was pleasant about Ethan's silliness, and his soothing words sounded right, but she'd never seen a knight protector disagree with a man of God, let alone call him out in the middle of a service. Lauren also did not understand the unexpected wink the Knight had given her and her brothers as he'd left. He'd acted strangely, perhaps, but he didn't seem evil.

As quietly as possible, the three children hurried out the inner doors and into the entryway, where the two acolytes stood, shaking their heads disapprovingly. One of the young men held a finger to his lips while the other motioned for them to sit in some chairs off to the side.

"But—" Ethan started, then glanced at Lauren, who shook her head. She didn't want to create another scene.

Gradually, other parishioners filed out of the church—the first wave of people left in a hurry, without the usual after-church banter. No one would make eye contact with the children. As Lauren sat in the entryway outside the chapel, she shivered, mulling over the hard questions about good and evil.

The parson could help her figure this out. It was clear the bishop and the knight protector were at odds. So, who was right? Who was really representing the Light? She wished the parson was here; he would know.

Lauren heard the bishop inside the chapel, chatting with the remaining parishioners. The acolyte in the yellow robe went back into the sanctuary, while the one wearing the purple robe stayed with the children. The crowd leaving slowed to a trickle.

Aiden turned to the purple-robed acolyte and asked, "Can we go now?"

"I'm hungry, and it's a long walk home," Ethan added, scrunching up his face in his most pitiful look.

"Children, that is no way to address an Acolyte of the Violet Order," huffed the boy whose bruise had been healed. "You may address me as Brother Acolyte or Acolyte of the Violet Order, sir. Clearly, your parents have failed to teach civility in other areas besides proper behavior in church." His chin lifted. "Also, the bishop would like to talk to you about your parents," announced the acolyte, his tone uncaring and flat. He seemed to have recovered all the dignity he'd lost earlier when he'd been sprawled on the floor with a frog sitting on his head.

Despite the apparent coldness in his manner, he pulled some beef jerky from a pocket and offered it to the boys. "This should tide you over until the bishop is done."

The boys looked wide-eyed at Lauren as if to say please.

Lauren was still thinking through the comment about their parents. How did the acolytes and the bishop know who their parents were? However, if he did know something, she wanted to know what it was. She sat up straight. "Boys, we will wait for the bishop. Go ahead and eat the jerky."

The boys took what the acolyte offered, biting off pieces and gnawing on the tough meat. As more parishioners left the chapel, Lauren puzzled over why no one acknowledged the children's presence. Were people just mad at them for Sparkle Frog's antics and their subsequent laughter, or was there something else, something darker, behind them, being ignored by people who had previously been so warm to them?

Lauren hugged her arms, feeling more and more insecure. She realized that only two of the families that attended today had children, and theirs were very young. A strange sensation crept along Lauren's spine; it seemed as if the church had divided down some invisible line that she couldn't quite explain.

Finally, the bishop escorted the last parishioner out of the door and then came toward them. With a wave of his hand, the bishop sent away the Acolyte of the Violet Order.

The bishop smiled. "It is so good to see how you've kept your spirits high despite your troubling circumstances."

"Your Holiness, sir, how do you know who we are?" Lauren made sure to speak in a respectful tone. "We've never met you." To focus on her manners, she sat straight, her hands folded in her lap.

The bishop peered down at Lauren. "I am a bishop, my dear child. It's my job to know the happenings in my territory. How could I not know of the tragedy that has befallen the family of the knight protector of the Tower of Light?"

The children sat up straight at the honor the bishop appeared to bestow on their family as he squatted to their level. "In fact, part of the reason I have come to this Heathlands chapel is that I have reports that your mother is missing as well."

Ethan leapt from his seat. "Mama's not missing! Somebody's got her trapped in the dark!"

"Child!" the bishop scolded in a stern voice. "It is never acceptable to interrupt an elder! A child must first seek permission to speak and in a manner respecting their elder's position." The bishop grabbed Ethan by his upper arms and pulled him close. "I allowed the incident with the frog to go without discipline because the outcome produced more good than harm to the congregation. However, it's clear you've not been given proper instruction." The bishop shoved Ethan away. "Go stand in that corner."

Ethan turned pale and silent, but he walked woodenly to the corner and stuck his nose in it. Lauren was shocked by this sudden turn in attitude by the bishop. He seemed so kind in the service. Now he was just plain cruel.

Ethan let out a muffled whine. "My face doesn't fit."

"Silence, child!" the bishop barked. As he turned back to Lauren and Aiden, his fearsome expression melted into calm, as if the incident with Ethan had not occurred. "Despite their best efforts to keep your mother from running headlong into danger, the Mighty Mercenaries have lost contact with her. With both parents missing, there is a great concern for the Tower of Light." The bishop stood up and motioned out the window as if pointing toward the tower. "While its power naturally keeps the Darkness at bay, it's vulnerable to vandalism without someone to guard and protect it."

Aiden perked up. "We can guard it! We have magic weapons. Mine is a fiery sword."

"I'm sure you have all kinds of magic," the bishop assured in a patronizing tone. "What is needed now is more than good intentions and your active imagination. Did I not already have to reprimand your brother about asking permission properly before speaking?" The bishop stood and pointed to another corner of the room. "In fact, you go there now and contemplate the ways to show proper respect for your elders."

Lauren could no longer sit still and watch her brothers being punished for speaking the truth. She again clasped her hands and faced the bishop. "Good Bishop, may I speak, Your Holiness, sir?" She spoke formally while looking down at her hands and only sneaking peeks at her elder.

"Yes, child." The bishop held his head high, not bothering to make eye contact with her. It made Lauren feel like he thought he was some kind of king and she was a lowly servant. "What would you like to say?"

"The boys aren't imagining things." She raised her chin. "We do have magic weapons: a shield, a sword, and a spear! Also, we've all seen Mother in a dream, trapped in a dark place."

"I repeat what I said earlier." The bishop shook his head in disapproval. "You children clearly lack proper instruction. I know now that I must arrange for your care myself, or your overactive imaginations will be the death of you."

From the pocket of his robe, the bishop pulled out a paper and unrolled it.

On it, Lauren saw their father's seal. How did this stranger have a document with Father's seal?

With a sweep of his hand, the bishop pointed to the paper. "Your father left instructions that should he and your mother perish or be lost to the Darkness, you are to be taken to your grandparents in Fair Fields." He stepped toward the sanctuary and waved the acolytes to him with the flick of his wrist. "It will take time to prepare for your journey. In the meantime, you children have demonstrated you need supervision. The Acolyte of the Violet Order will stay at your house. He will assist you in maintaining your farm and the Tower of Light, not to mention enforcing discipline in your home."

Lauren went numb. She'd thought talking to the clergy might help her understand what was going on, but tension inside her told her this wasn't a good idea. Nothing the bishop had said had given her insight into who she could trust. In fact, his words left her more confused. She couldn't understand how the bishop had a paper with Father's seal.

The acolytes walked back toward them, and she realized the thought of having strangers at the house didn't seem right to her, either.

"Good Bishop, Your Holiness, sir." Lauren tried to keep a quiver out of her voice. "I don't think Mother and Father would approve of strangers in our house. The parson said he would organize church families to help us, and he himself brought us food." Lauren kept her eyes downcast, again focused on her folded hands.

"Oh, child." The bishop shook his head as if she were a little baby. "You can't begin to comprehend the danger. Did you see the parson today? And where were those families you expected to help?" The bishop again squatted down to her level, making her feel small. "Good people are disappearing. Our knight protectors are sowing dissension. What more must happen for you to understand how far the Darkness has spread?" The bishop put his hands on Lauren's shoulders. "The Tower of Light is a key target for those wishing to spread the Darkness. I insist that my acolyte watches over you until we can make more permanent arrangements."

With a haughty look, the bishop stood and pointed at the violet acolyte. "Never fear. The Acolyte of the Violet Order will be given a mighty battle horn that it is said even the hounds of hell respect. He will go home with you now." He turned to Mr. Yellow Robe. "The Acolyte of the Dandelion Order will be on standby, ready to come and

assist as needed." With a sigh, the bishop glanced, first at
Ethan's corner, then toward the one where Aiden stood.
"You might show a little gratitude for receiving a helper to
your farm."

Lauren thought about all that had happened, trying to
do what was best for her brothers, who stood in their
respective corners. She didn't like a single thing about the
way the bishop conducted himself this morning. Despite all
he'd said in the sermon, he didn't seem one bit tolerant of
children, but without the parson or her parents to talk to,
Lauren didn't know what choice she had. She couldn't
figure out an option besides obeying the bishop. Besides,
they really could use some help with the chores. Would this
purple-robed snob be of assistance?

Lauren suppressed her doubts. "It's nice to meet you,
Mr. Acolyte, sir. My name is Lauren." She pointed to the
corners. And these are my brothers, Aiden and Ethan."

The Acolyte gave a curt nod in their direction, and
Lauren continued, "Mr. Acolyte, sir, you may accompany
us home. However, I'll have to ask that you stay in the
barn. Our parents would not approve of strangers in the
house."

The acolyte opened his mouth, possibly to protest,
when Ethan cut him off by whining from the corner, "Mr.
Bishop, sir. Can I get out now?"

The bishop turned red and looked like he might
explode. "All of you may go." With a flourish of his
crimson robes, he left the entryway.

Eager to breathe fresh air, the children hurried outside.
The Acolyte of the Violet Order darted back in and
reemerged with a leather pack and a belt slung over his

shoulder. Attached to the belt was a hand ax, which looked more like a tool than a weapon, and a black ram's horn.

The acolyte walked ahead of the children, and Lauren took a better look at the horn. It appeared to be made of a black ram's horn, and its raised surfaces had been dry-brushed white. It had an image of a large battle with armored men on horseback being devoured by beastly hounds. An unsettling feeling spread from her stomach and began to take over her limbs. She'd never known anything of the Light to allow such darkness. How could she and this acolyte, who was really a boy not much older than she was, repel the forces of the Dark One?

8. The Acolyte of the Violet Order

As the children walked home, Aiden was really confused about what had just transpired. He got that Lauren was just trying to get them out of a sticky situation, but this didn't feel right to him. He turned back toward the church. "Sissy, look behind us! The sky still isn't right. Why hasn't it lightened up?"

The Violet acolyte swelled with pride. "The bishop says the Darkness is spreading. Soon, the twilight will bathe all of Zoura. That's why the bishop's here. If you notice, the haze fades just outside the church. This concerns the bishop greatly."

"Let me see if I understand." Aiden took the lead as the acolyte didn't know where to turn toward their home. "The bishop thinks the Darkness has spread to the church, and he's trying to figure out how that could have happened?"

Aiden began walking backward to continue the conversation. He knew this road like the back of his hand, and there was something shifty about this guy. He wanted to get the whole story.

The acolyte nodded at Aiden's assertion, his expression earnest. "Something like that."

Ethan tugged on the acolyte's robe, asking, "Hey, what's your real name?"

"As I said before and is evident by the color of my robe, I am an Acolyte of the Violet Order." The acolyte removed Ethan's hand from his robe as if Ethan had cooties.

"So that's really your name? You don't have a normal name like Steve or Bob?" Ethan asked incredulously.

The acolyte stopped short and squatted down to look Ethan directly in the eyes. "I gave up that part of myself when I swore my oath. As I already explained, you can address me as Brother Acolyte or Acolyte of the Violet Order."

"Violet?" Ethan had an odd look on his face. "Violet's a flower. Your robe is purple and green."

"Violet is a shade of purple, boy." The acolyte acted frustrated by the whole line of questioning as he stood back up and continued walking. "If you were educated, you would know that. The green tassels represent the new life brought by the order."

"So, you're dressed up like a flower?" Ethan quipped as he skipped around the older boy.

"Most certainly not." The acolyte whirled about to correct Ethan. "Watch yourself, young man. Because I am an Acolyte of the Violet Order and your elder, you should address me with respect."

They had nearly reached the bridge to cross the stream. There sat Sparkle Frog at the edge of the bridge as if waiting for Ethan, who ran ahead to greet his animal friend. "OK, Brother Flower, whatever you say." Sarcasm laced Ethan's tone.

Aiden suppressed a snicker. He thought the name Brother Flower was just about right for this pretentious snob. He didn't look like he'd done any real work in his life. How was he going to help them on the farm?

Aiden turned to get his bearing on the road, and when he turned back, Lauren caught the acolyte's attention and asked, "So what does an acolyte do?"

The acolyte, apparently ready to impress Lauren with his responsibilities, took quick steps to catch up with her. "It means I am training to be a member of the clergy. I study the Good Book and assist the bishop with his work." He looked down his nose at Lauren as if to make sure she was paying attention. "After I have shown the proper attitude, skills, and devotion, I will be given the opportunity to advance to the order of the dandelion robes."

Lauren nodded, following along with his words. Aiden wondered if that meant the other acolyte could boss Brother Flower around.

"Eventually, I will progress into the order of the rose robes, which signifies a fully trained and qualified clergy." The acolyte raised his chin, which accentuated a smug look. "I will have a church of my own."

As they walked to the middle of the bridge, Aiden asked, "So, was the parson part of the order of the rose robes?"

"Absolutely not!" The violet acolyte replied in disgust. "He was merely a parson, someone of the laity over the standard congregation, given a position to fill a gap." The acolyte shook his head. "He completed none of the rigorous training and tests I am undergoing." He pointed to his chest in a way that emphasized his importance. "The parson was in his position for far too long. He should have been relieved years ago by a properly trained clergyman. His presence might explain the odd way in which the Darkness has spread here."

This explanation surprised Aiden and added to the confusion of the day. "So, you think the parson has something to do with the Darkness spreading here?"

"I don't know that for sure. The Darkness is coming to all parts of Zoura, so the parson may have nothing to do with it, but you saw for yourself how the Darkness covers even the church." Brother Acolyte pointed back toward the church.

Uneasiness settled deeper in Aiden's bones. Never had the encroachment of the Darkness seemed so apparent. Granted, the last few weeks had been cloudy, but he hadn't noticed the extent of the odd, dark sky. That surprised Aiden the most as he tracked the weather like an almanac.

Conversation ebbed as Ethan again raced ahead of the others. With Ethan's laughter and Sparkle Frog's croaking in the distance, Aiden turned to face the direction of travel and had time to think about all that had happened.

As they neared home, Ethan about-faced, running at top speed, and nearly knocked over Aiden. "I think I heard something."

"Slow down, little brother. You almost mowed me over." Aiden struggled to get his feet back under him. "Now, what did you say?"

Ethan sputtered, "I dunno. I heard someping."

Worrying about a possible intruder made everybody more cautious as they approached the house. Soon they all heard a banging sound coming from the opposite side of the house. Aiden pressed his finger against his lips as if to say be quiet, then motioned for everybody to get off the path and go down the hill toward the stream. Aiden looked back to see if they were following. The acolyte looked confused, as though he didn't understand, so Lauren mouthed the word "trouble" and followed Aiden.

The acolyte shifted his weight from one foot to the other as if he had a moment of indecision. Then he grabbed the dark horn from its place on the strap over his right shoulder, ready to blow it at any moment, and followed the children.

The four of them crept single file along the stream edge, hidden from the view of the barnyard. As they got closer to the path which would lead from the kitchen to the stream, there was a quack. Lauren hoped she was just hearing things.

Daddy Duck usually spelled trouble.

Apparently, the acolyte heard it, too, because he hissed, "What was that noise?"

Before Lauren could answer, there was a flash, and a quacking Daddy Duck plopped onto the acolyte's full head of curly hair as if he planned to make a nest. The children tried their best not to laugh as the acolyte let go of the horn and waved his arms, screaming, "Get off!"

Despite the acolyte's efforts, Daddy Duck kept flying off and then landing again on the acolyte's head.

The sight was so funny that Ethan forgot he was supposed to be respectful. "He wants to be your friend, Brother Flower." He used his teasing tone. "Right, Aiden?"

"Yes. Daddy Duck's just being friends, Brother Flower," Aiden explained as he began to laugh.

The acolyte continued to flail about. "Friends or not, *I* just want him off!"

Aiden took a deep breath and suppressed his laugh, "If you hold still, I'll help." After another moment of flailing about, the acolyte finally did what Aiden suggested and followed his motions to squat down.

Aiden carefully took Daddy Duck off the boy's head and set him in the nearby stream. Daddy Duck paddled away.

"Hey, listen!" Ethan cupped his hand to his ear. "That banging stopped!"

They ran up the hill, not sure what to expect.

At the bottom of the Tower of Light was a board the size of a ladder rung attached by two nails to each side of the doorframe. A second board hung knee-high from the ground, with nails driven in on one side. There was a large claw hammer lying on the ground in front of the tower door as if someone had just stopped work.

Aiden felt his eyes get big. Had someone tried to board up the Tower of Light, and if so, who had done it?

The acolyte stepped closer, his hand shading his eyes. He shook his head, "It wasn't like that when you left, was it? You didn't try to protect it yourselves, did you?" He asked in an accusing tone.

"No, of course not!" Aiden spat back. This guy was a real piece of work. First, he couldn't figure out that Daddy Duck was just playing, and then he couldn't figure out that the banging noise was somebody hammering boards on the tower.

Aiden looked the tower up and down, then turned to see that the acolyte's gaze was focused between the house and the barn toward a big oak tree on the edge of the forest, where something fluttered in the breeze. A feeling of dread spread out from his stomach as it felt like it had dropped to the ground. Whatever they saw was a clue to the mystery of the boards. But was it a trap?

A brown cloak, looking much like the one worn by the knight protector, waved from one of the oak's lower limbs. Its bottom was tattered and full of holes, with leaves stuck to it.

In silence, the group moved toward the oak tree. Ethan realized that Daddy Duck must have been warning them about trouble around the corner. Ethan saw the Acolyte grip his dark horn so tightly that his knuckles turned white. This scared Ethan because if a big boy like Brother Flower was scared, it must be serious.

When they reached the tree, Ethan couldn't see anyone around. As he looked at the cloak, it reminded him of his Father wearing it when he brought home wild game in the winter. This thought gave him momentary courage that he could be like Father someday. Ethan pulled on the cloak until it fell from the branch. Then he wrapped it around his shoulders. His little six-year-old frame was buried in the large cloak, but he beamed and stuck out his chest. "Look at me," he crowed. "I'm the knight protector, Brother Flower! He really conked your wonkus earlier."

All the tension and frustration of the morning finally came to a head at the sound of Ethan's mocking words. "Take that off, you silly little child." The acolyte's tone turned scornful. "You look ridiculous. And for the last time, stop calling me Brother Flower."

"Fine." Ethan gripped the cloak, then smoothed it onto the ground and slowly began to fold it up.

Ethan looked up and saw Lauren scanning the woods in earnest. Then she asked, "Um, should we maybe search for the owner?"

The acolyte whirled around, his face almost as purple as his cloak. "'Um' is most improper, young girl. We need to get into the house. It's time for lunch."

"But you gave us food at the chapel. We're not hungry!" Ethan complained as he picked up the cloak and tucked it under his arm.

"That little bit of jerky I was so kind to share was hardly lunch. You can't fool me into thinking you aren't hungry. You're going to eat lunch now." The acolyte harrumphed and marched toward the house. "Come!"

Ethan had seen grown-ups in this state before. He knew there would be no arguing with him, and he did have a point. If the knight protector really was a bad guy, the kids would need their weapons to defeat him. Lauren must have been thinking the same thing because she turned back to Aiden and Ethan and said, "Come on, boys. Let's go."

Aiden looked like he might protest, but Lauren just shook her head, and he seemed to get the point that this wasn't the time to argue. They all followed the acolyte to the house.

As they got close to the house, Aiden paused to look toward the tower. "Something doesn't make sense. If the knight protector wanted to do something bad to the Tower of Light, why would he go to the trouble of boarding it up?"

"What do you mean?" the acolyte asked his hands on his hips. "Wouldn't blocking access to the Tower of Light prevent you from adding oil to the lamp? Wouldn't it just die out? I don't know of any lamp that can shine more than a few hours without tending."

It would have made more sense just to take the lantern. Aiden looked up at the older boy with a questioning look on his face. "Don't you know? The lantern doesn't need tending. The lamp stays lit on its own. Father says that as long as there are people who love God's truth and will stand for it, then the Light will shine forever."

Since the acolyte looked perplexed, Ethan piped in, "We don't tend the Light. Sissy and Aiden read the Good Book, and we all say our prayers." He looked to Lauren for confirmation and felt relieved as she nodded. "You can't put the Light out, really. You can hide it, but you can't put it out. You know, like the song."

The acolyte looked even more confused. "What song?"

"You know, the song!" Ethan declared, getting very exasperated with this boy who clearly wasn't as smart as he said he was. "This little light of mine, I'm gonna let it shine." He sang all the verses, then ended with, "Won't let the Dark One blow it out. I'm gonna let it shine. Let it shine, let it shine, let it shine."

The surprised look on the acolyte's face told Ethan that he had never heard the song. Ethan's brow furrowed with concern. "How did you get to be so important if you don't know about Light of Mine?"

The acolyte defensively jutted his jaw. "It's entirely juvenile. The order is concerned with more important things than children's songs."

"That 'children's song' sheds an interesting light on our current very grown-up situation, don't you think?" Lauren asked pointedly.

87

"What—what are you insinuating?" The acolyte got all huffy.

"I think Aiden's onto something." Changing the subject, Lauren pointed to the tower. "If whoever's messing with the tower wanted to help the Darkness, he would have just taken the lantern and tried to destroy it. If not for that, he would have shuttered the tower windows and then blocked the door. You know, blow out the Light or hide it under a bushel."

The acolyte took a deep breath and slowly let it out. "That's an interesting theory, young girl. However, you are missing the most obvious answer. Whoever it was, knight protector or otherwise may just have been quite crazy in the head."

He turned away from the children dismissively and approached the front door of the house, then wheeled about. "Doesn't my theory much better explain the odd behavior than anything you are proposing? In my studies, scholars are quick to show that generally, the most obvious answer is the right one."

Lauren paused, turned to the tower, then back to the acolyte. "You may have a point."

Ethan wasn't convinced and was about to object again when Aiden chimed in, "I guess that could be right, but just because someone goes crazy doesn't mean they're stupid. All this person did was make it really hard for him or anybody else to access the Light."

The acolyte paused and looked at Aiden. "Yes, young one, often going mad is accompanied by the loss of reasoning skills."

"We're all a little out of sorts," said Lauren, wanting to stop the debate…at least for now. "Why don't we just get some lunch and figure things out." She went into the house through the kitchen door.

The boys ran in after her, but the acolyte stayed on the porch.

"Brother Acolyte," Lauren said, "you may eat with us. I don't think Mother would disapprove of that hospitality."

He stepped through the door.

Lauren approached the stove and scooped the ashes off the top of the spider pot, which she pulled out of the smoldering coals and set on the table. She took the lid off and set the pot on a hot pad on the kitchen counter. The boys got bowls and spoons while she grabbed a wooden spoon and stirred the oatmeal.

Ethan climbed into his chair. He saw Meow-Meow come into the room and try to rub up against Lauren's ankles, but Lauren nudged him away as she carried cups of water to the table. Meow-Meow next approached Aiden, but he, too, was busy putting bowls on the table. The only person standing still was the acolyte. Meow-Meow approached warily, not sure if this new person was a friend or foe.

Ethan was really wondering the same thing.

The acolyte kept staring at Lauren, then the boys, acting all huffy. Finally, he asked, "What are you doing?"

"Getting lunch." Lauren struggled to keep the exasperation out of her voice. "Isn't that what you told us to do?"

"That's definitely not lunch," the acolyte retorted. "I saw the smokehouse out back, so you must have ham or some bacon." He pointed toward the cupboard. "This is a farm, isn't it? Don't you have potatoes? Now get the fire going and make a proper meal."

The children stood stock-still, their mouths open. In all his life, Ethan had never eaten a cooked meal on the Sabbath. Mama and Daddy always said it was the Lord's Day and that they were to spend it resting and thinking about Him.

They made sure the animals were taken care of, but Ethan's parents didn't even eat themselves until sundown on the Sabbath. Mama said that oatmeal or porridge for breakfast and lunch was a mercy for her little ones, but someday they should fast, too.

"What on earth is the matter with you?" the acolyte asked. "You look at me as though I've sprouted two heads. The youngest acolytes always make the meals on the Sabbath. You clearly made porridge. What I'm asking for is no harder. Hop to it."

The children stood silently. Ethan wondered what Sissy would do. Was this stranger really the boss of them? How would she explain the rules to somebody who should already know them anyway?

Meanwhile, Meow-Meow worked up the courage to creep closer to the acolyte and was only inches away from his legs. The kitten's head turned from side to side, matching the rhythm of the tassels swaying at the bottom of the acolyte's robe.

Lauren stepped forward. "Since you're not from here, I can understand you not knowing our song, but how can you not know about keeping the Sabbath?"

"Oh, that." The acolyte shook his head dismissively. "Child, when you have studied the Good Book as I have, under the tutelage of the best scholars, you begin to understand what it really means." He put his hand to his chest and sighed. "The strict rules of the Old Book do not apply to us believers of the New Book. We are unbound from the rules of the first followers of God."

The acolyte pointed to the Good Book next to Father's chair in the great room. "If you knew your Good Book well, you'd know that even the Savior 'worked' on the Sabbath by healing a man." He made a shooing motion with his hands. "Go! Do what I asked so we can have a proper meal."

"Daddy wouldn't like this." Ethan squared his shoulders and made fists. "I don't know about all the things you're talking about, but I'm not going to do something Daddy wouldn't like."

"Me, neither," Aiden declared, stepping between Ethan and the acolyte. Ethan was proud of his big brother for stepping up to defend him.

"I'm with my brothers," Lauren said as she stepped next to Aiden and put a hand on his shoulder in support. "You didn't get the point of the story about the Savior's healing on the Sabbath. Father told us, when he read it to us, that the religious leaders were trying to trap the Savior. They wanted an excuse to hurt Him."

Lauren walked over to the Good Book, picked it up, and handed it to the acolyte. "Healing the man had to be God's will, or the Savior wouldn't have done it on the Sabbath. Show me where it is God's will that we break the Sabbath so you can have pork and potatoes."

As Lauren was speaking, Meow-Meow crouched, ready to pounce. The acolyte stepped forward menacingly, which set his robe tassels swaying at a frenetic pace. Meow-Meow leapt at one of the little balls. His first jump missed, but then he rolled onto his back and began to beat the tassels back and forth with his paws.

Ethan had a clear line of sight to Meow-Meow's antics and tried but failed to hold in his giggles. Aiden must have seen the same thing as he broke out in laughter as well.

The acolyte stopped short and looked behind him. "What are you boys laughing at? This conversation is not funny. Besides, you will show me respect!"

The boys just pointed and laughed.

Again, the acolyte turned around, but he apparently still couldn't see Meow-Meow, who'd crept under his robe, batting at the tassels with all his catlike might.

Finally, Lauren let out a chuckle, then stepped toward the acolyte. Then she bent down next to the confused acolyte and picked up the mischievous kitty. The acolyte was still their guest and didn't need a cat harassing him.

"Meow-Meow likes your flowers, Brother Flower," teased Ethan.

The acolyte's face turned red as if he were about to explode, but then he about-faced, pulled what looked like a hard roll out of his pack, walked outside, and stood in the yard under the light of the tower.

The children exhaled a collective sigh of relief. "Who's my good kitty?" Lauren asked Meow-Meow and scratched under his chin.

"I don't like that guy," declared Aiden with a scowl. "He's always bossing us around, and he's got weird ideas."

"Yeah, Sissy," Ethan said. "How do we get rid of him?"

Sighing, Lauren put Meow-Meow down and began to dish out oatmeal. "We'll have to suffer through today and see what happens. I'm not comfortable with this, either. I hope Mother comes home soon. She said she'd be home today."

The children ate their oatmeal in silence and then proceeded to the great room to read the Good Book, which was their custom after lunch on the Sabbath. Lauren found their father's reading list with the passage for the day:

> If someone warns you that this meat has been offered to idols, then don't eat it for the sake of the man who told you and of his conscience. In this case, his feeling about it is the important thing, not yours.

As she was reading, the acolyte crept inside and joined them in the great room.

Lauren shut the book.

The acolyte stepped forward, his head down. "I'm sorry for my behavior, children. I was guilty of not respecting your conscience, as the passage says. I was acting proud, and I am very sorry. Please forgive my transgression."

Ethan looked at Aiden and saw him cock his head and raise an eyebrow. Aiden must have been just as surprised by this turnaround. An apology was the very last thing he expected from the acolyte.

"It's all right." Lauren stepped close and patted him on the shoulder. "This is a stressful situation."

"Thank you for your grace." The acolyte removed Lauren's hand from his shoulder. "What other family traditions do you observe on the Sabbath?"

"Usually a lot of naps," Ethan grumbled, not very happy about the prospect of being forced to take a nap.

"We try to play quietly so Mother and Father can rest. Sometimes we go to the creek." Aiden got an expectant look.

"Well, then, let's go … unless you want a nap." The acolyte winked at Ethan.

"Wait!" Lauren thrust her hands on her hips. "You boys need to change out of your nice clothes."

"OK, Sissy," the boys moaned in unison, then hurried up to the loft. When Ethan came back down, he sized up the acolyte. He wasn't sure he could believe the sudden change. With how mean the acolyte was and the way he didn't even know "Light of Mine," Ethan wondered if the acolyte was really working for the Dark One. If he was from the Dark One, then he wouldn't play nice, would he? Ethan guessed there was only one way to find out. "Come on, Brother Flower. Let's play." Ethan rushed out the front door toward the creek.

Halfway to the creek, Lauren asked the acolyte, "Where are you from?"

"I was born on the east coast in a small town you would not know of. When I was about your age, I began my studies at the Cathedral of Emoh'nomed, far away from my tiny birth town." The acolyte wistfully looked off to the east. "Initially, I was a part of the cohort Syug'Dab. Eventually, I was chosen to enter the Order of the Violet Robe."

"Why did your parents send you away to study?" Lauren asked hesitantly.

"They didn't." Pain tightened the muscles in the acolyte's face. "My parents both died of the plague and left me an orphan."

"That's terrible!" cried Lauren, horrified at the thought of anyone losing their mother and father. Her breath caught. What if ... something terrible happened to her own father ... and mother?

"That's so sad." Ethan's voice softened as he tried to hug the acolyte.

The acolyte stood awkwardly as if unsure how to respond to affection, then bent down to hug Ethan back.

They walked in silence after that, not running as usual, perhaps because of the acolyte's sad story. Nearing the creek, they noticed that a hushed silence had fallen over the forest, almost as if the animals were collectively holding their breath. Even the locusts and crickets kept quiet.

They reached the edge of the creek, spring-fed from a source further up the valley, yet not too far away from their farm. The water looked crystal clear, as always.

Sparkle Frog sat patiently on the edge of the creek. As soon as Ethan approached, the frog leapt high and splashed into the water—a sound that joyously broke the hush.

Ethan rushed into the creek and waded toward Sparkle Frog; his arms extended to catch the wild hopper. While the others watched and laughed, the boy and the frog splashed around without a care in the world. They laughed harder and frolicked more intensely, gradually moving downstream toward the point where a larger stream from the east flowed into the creek.

The others stayed on the side of the shore. From Lauren's vantage point, she had a much better view of the eastern-sourced stream. Her eyes on her brother, Lauren shouted, "Ethan, come back! The stream is much too swift. Stay in the creek."

Ethan paused and turned around, but Sparkle Frog continued toward the wider stream. "Aah, Sissy, I'll be fine. I can swim." He turned his back to Lauren and followed the frog.

"I don't want to have to rescue you, little man." Lauren's hands went on her hips. "Come back here!"

"Look!" Aiden shouted as he pointed to where the two waterways came together.

Lauren's gaze tracked the direction Aiden indicated, and she caught sight of something odd. Where the two channels joined was typical watery turbulence, but instead of being just choppy water, it looked as if the two bodies of water were mixing different liquids. While the creek had still, clear water, the stream appeared gray with streaks of black, giving the water an ominous look.

Lauren patted the acolyte's shoulder to make sure she had his attention and pointed to the disturbance. "Mr. Acolyte, sir, does that water look normal to you?"

"No, it doesn't." The acolyte's expression turned darker than the polluted water. "Something is very, very wrong." He cupped his hands around his mouth and shouted, "Ethan, can you hear me? Get away from where the waters merge!"

Ignoring the warning, Ethan waded faster and frolicked harder toward the merger, his strides creating wakes, but Sparkle Frog began to swim toward the bank, only further down, close to the water's confluence.

"Ethan!" the acolyte again yelled. "Stop! Something's wrong!"

His breath was wasted. Ethan continued toward the larger stream.

The acolyte leapt into the creek, swam with quick strokes to Ethan, scooped him up, and threw him over his shoulder like a sack of potatoes. His breath heaved as he waded through the water with Ethan clinging to his neck. Though he wobbled, he finally stepped up onto the solid ground. Ethan and the acolyte were safe!

"Brother Flower put me down!" Ethan kicked and writhed. "You're mean. Let me go!" He pounded the acolyte on his back. As the acolyte set Ethan onto his feet, Ethan yelled, "Why did you do that? You're not my daddy. You can't tell me what to do."

"Look at the frog. Over there!" The acolyte pointed toward a bank downstream, past where the stream and creek met.

As the children and the acolyte watched, a swift current swept up Sparkle Frog and slammed him against a rock near the bank. His brilliant rainbow of colors had faded to a dingy gray.

"Aww, poor Sparkle Frog," Ethan's voice caught as tears began to form, and he rushed along the bank. Lauren knew how much Ethan loved Sparkle Frog. Given how Father said he was of the Light, she couldn't understand what was happening to the poor amphibian.

"He looks … dead," Aiden stammered as they all caught up with Ethan and hurried toward the frog. "What are we going to do?"

"Let's not rush." As the acolyte knelt on the bank by the rock Sparkle Frog clung to, the children huddled around him. Up close, they could see the frog's skin moving in and out. He was still breathing.

The acolyte bent over and studied Sparkle Frog. "The water coming in from the east looks polluted." The acolyte shook his head. "Frogs are particularly susceptible to toxins." He reached toward Sparkle Frog as if to stroke his skin.

"Wait!" Lauren cried. "Don't touch him! If someone has dumped poison in the water, it could sicken you, too."

Ethan began to wail in earnest, with tears raining from his red eyes. Aiden put a comforting arm around his little brother, and Ethan turned into his shoulder, which muffled his cries.

The acolyte nodded. "That would explain the funny color." He searched along the shoreline, picking up, then discarding a clump of leaves that had apparently washed ashore. "If I can find something suitable, we can wrap the little frog up and carry him to a place where we can take care of him."

Ethan turned from Aiden, sniffled up his tears, and encouraged the acolyte. "Hurry, Mr. Acolyte, sir," Ethan cried. "Don't let Sparkle Frog die!"

The acolyte yanked off his drenched robe and stood before them in khaki pants like Aiden's. He knelt on the bank and carefully bent over to wrap the ailing frog in the heavy wool. He stood back up and carried his precious cargo to the pool that formed the head of the creek, then gently laid the frog into the water and rinsed him off, using the edge of his robe as a washcloth.

Lauren thought one of Sparkle Frog's limbs twitched, but his countenance remained unchanged.

"I don't understand," moaned Aiden, deep concern in his voice. "You washed the dark stuff off. Shouldn't getting rid of the Darkness help Sparkle Frog?"

"Please, Sparkle Frog, don't die." Tears streamed down Ethan's face. "Get better, please."

"Maybe he needs time to recover." Lauren put her arm around Ethan to console him.

"You might be right." The acolyte placed the still-limp frog on a large rock near the shore.

"Sissy, pray," Ethan demanded, stifling his sobs.

Lauren bowed her head. "Dear Lord, please help Sparkle Frog get better. We don't know what all this

Darkness is about, but we know You can make it go away. Amen."

"Oh, look!" Ethan jumped to his feet, his back to them.

Suddenly there was a familiar flap of wings and a brilliant flash of light as Daddy Duck flew in from the east. For the briefest instant, a bright beam of light originating at the lantern in the Tower of Light appeared to bounce off the white spot on Daddy Duck's forehead to pierce the forest shade and spotlight Sparkle Frog. In that instant, they both shined with more brilliant color than they had before.

"Wow!" cried Ethan. The others stood open-mouthed but silent.

As suddenly as it had come, the light disappeared. With a loud croak, Sparkle Frog jumped from the rock and landed neatly on Ethan's head.

Slack-jawed, the acolyte clapped his hand against his cheek. "I've never seen anything like that! How did you do that?"

"What do you mean?" asked Aiden, apparently confused by the acolyte's question.

The acolyte shrugged. "Never have I prayed and seen such instantaneous results, nor have I seen power like that. It ... it was a miracle!" The acolyte stepped away from the children, looking at them with a combination of respect and awe.

"You're joking, right?" asked Lauren, shocked that someone of the clergy had never seen the Light perform a miracle.

"This is no joke, young lady. I've never seen prayer answered in that way," he said defensively.

"Are you sure you know the same God we do?" Aiden asked. "Sparkle Frog healed you this morning. Did you pray after you got hurt?"

"Well, not exactly like this," the Acolyte responded. "I mean, healing the bump on my head wasn't exactly what I was seeking help from the Almighty for."

"But that's what happened, and it turned out OK, right?" Aiden responded.

The acolyte nodded mutely, apparently at a complete loss for words.

Ethan chimed in, "This kind of thing happens all the time. Daddy says if we have a need, we pray. God takes care of it."

Lauren was about to interject but then paused in thought. *Well, maybe not every time, and it's not always with a bright light from the tower. Still, this guy acts like God doesn't make things work for His good.*

"I don't know what to say." The acolyte found a felled tree and sat down heavily. "Maybe it's because you live so close to the Tower of Light that you experience such things. Until today, I've never witnessed such miracles." The acolyte kept shaking his head. He looked ashen like Sparkle Frog had before the miracle had healed him.

"Do you think that black stuff in the water made Sparkle Frog sick?" Ethan asked.

Both Lauren and the acolyte nodded.

"So, where did it come from?" Ethan stared back toward the swirling area where the waters met. "If it's bad stuff, we need to stop it so Sparkle Frog doesn't get sick again."

"Maybe we should check it out. We could stop it if the origin isn't that far away," Lauren said.

"It could be dangerous." The acolyte picked up his robe and wrung the water from it. "I'm not sure we should go there on our own."

"We need to find out," Ethan said. "Sparkle Frog lives here. He won't understand to stay out of the dark water."

"Plus, if it's toxic for Sparkle Frog, it's likely toxic for everything that comes in contact with it," Lauren added.

"Please, Mr. Acolyte," Aiden begged. "Our windmill gets water from the creek. If the dark water in the stream backs up, our drinking water will be polluted."

"Fine. We will go investigate until I say it's time to turn back. I need you, children, to promise to turn back when I say so."

When they nodded their agreement, the acolyte waved a hand at Ethan as if to tell him to lead on.

Ethan let out a whoop, crossed the clear creek, and began walking along the edge of the polluted stream. Lauren hung back to see what the Acolyte would do next.

Before following Ethan, the older boy hung his robe on a tree branch to dry and set his pack there as well, but first, he retrieved his horn, which he hung from a leather strap over his left shoulder. He also found a fallen tree branch, about three feet long, and hefted it over his right shoulder, then crossed the stream to catch up with Ethan. Lauren followed him across the stream.

They proceeded quietly up the polluted stream as if lost in their own thoughts and wary of any dangers that might be in the forest, but other than an occasional bird call and the scurry of squirrels in the underbrush, there were few signs of life. Lauren took the lead because she had explored this area before. As they neared the source of the stream, they began to hear grunts like someone doing heavy labor.

Lauren put her finger to her lips; they slowed their movements and crept around a bend in the stream. She peeked through a large bush and into a sunlit patch of tall grass that extended uphill to their left with the stream running to their right and paused. The knight protector stood a few paces away with his back to them, kicking the end of a terra cotta pipe. The acolyte stopped short behind her and blocked the boys' progress.

From Lauren's point of view, it looked as though the knight protector was trying to make the pipe settle into a freshly dug trench that had matted the tall grass down. A trickle of black liquid oozed from the end of the pipe and ran down the ditch to the source of the spring. Two other pipes lay next to the channel, waiting their turn to be put in place, which would extend the entire pipeline to the water. Once connected, the pipes would be a perfect channel for the black liquid.

The acolyte grabbed Lauren's arm and pulled as he stepped back behind the bush. She was shocked by this and twisted out of his grasp, which caused him to become off-balance and stumble back behind the bush. Aiden sidestepped to the edge of the creek so as not to be crushed by the falling acolyte. This gave Aiden a line of sight to the knight protector.

In an instant, Lauren realized the acolyte was trying to pull her away from danger, so she lunged toward Aiden to push him back beyond the bush.

Instead, Aiden deftly stepped forward into the clearing and shouted, "You stop that right NOW!"

Lauren took a tumble to her knees behind him, just barely avoiding toppling into the creek.

The knight protector whirled to look where Lauren and Aiden were clearly exposed. "Now, children," he said, "you don't understand."

"Wrong!" screamed the acolyte while rushing out from behind the bush. "*You* don't understand! How can you live with yourself, spreading the Darkness?" He dropped the tree branch club he'd had in his right hand and reached for his horn. "We'll put an end to you once and for all."

The knight protector's arm snapped back, then forward as he hurled a knife through the air. It cut through the strap holding the acolyte's horn and landed in the brush behind them.

"No!" cried the acolyte. He grabbed for the horn as it fell, but he missed. The horn thudded to the edge of the stream and began to float away.

Lauren was frozen with indecision. Should she try to block the knight protector or help retrieve the horn? The knight protector turned and ran up the far side of the trench and over the hill. By the time the acolyte recovered from the sudden attack and retrieved the horn from the stream, her view of the knight protector was obscured by the crest of the hill and the woods beyond.

The acolyte shook his head as he wiped leaves and dust off the horn. "Children," he said, his voice thick with disappointment, "much as I want to skin his hide, I don't think going after him is a good idea. Even if I send out a call for help, he'll have time to hide before the others arrive." The acolyte walked forward and crouched down next to the trench, peering at the pipes and trickle of dark water. "Let's focus on this. Perhaps it's something we can control."

Aiden walked over and looked around in the bushes where the knight protector's knife landed. He crawled under the brush and found the knife. Picking it up, he stood and lightly ran his finger along the edge. "Wow! This makes our knives look dull. And boy, did he have good aim."

"Put it down," Lauren demanded, then knelt near the acolyte. "Maybe we should try clogging up the channel to keep the poison out."

"With what?" Aiden squatted to get a closer look at the pipe.

"Rocks and mud, I guess," Lauren said.

"We can't get the black stuff on us," Aiden reminded them.

The children couldn't find any nearby rocks of sufficient size to block the pipe from connecting to the channel. There were some small pebbles in the pool, but their attempts to make a ball of mud and rocks to plug the pipeline ended with the black stuff still oozing out of the space left around the rocks.

"It isn't working," Lauren said. "The rocks aren't big enough, and the ooze is washing the plug away."

"How about using my stick?" asked Brother Flower.

"Yeah," said Ethan. "It's almost the same size as the pipe."

"We can put a big mud ball at the end of the pipeline and jam in the stick to make a blockage," Aiden said.

They worked together to execute Aiden's plan. Ethan made a ball out of the mud on the bank upstream of the dark ooze. Aiden picked it up, carried it to the end of the pipeline, and dropped it into the trench. Then the acolyte jammed the mud ball and the stick as far into the pipe as he could.

Immediately the flow stopped. Minutes later, the children gave a victory shout when the pool downstream lost its dull, dark tint.

"This is just a temporary fix." Lauren slapped her hands together to knock off the dirt. "The knight protector will return. We've got to find the source of the ooze and stop it."

"We have to fix it," Ethan said with a tremble in his voice. "Sparkle Frog could get sick again."

"Yeah, Sissy. Let's do it!" Aiden turned and took a step up the hill.

"Hold on!" The acolyte grabbed Aiden's shoulder. "I agree with your sister, but I don't feel I'm prepared right now to deal with whatever may be the source of this evil. I would be punished severely if I intentionally tried to chase down the knight protector with your children in tow. You three will be returning with me to the house." His eyes narrowed. "Now!"

Ethan looked up at the older boy with puppy dog eyes. "But what about Sparkle Frog? If he gets in the water again, he could get sick again, and we might not see."

"My first priority is to take care of you!" The acolyte pointed toward home and steered Ethan by the shoulder in that direction. "Let's go!"

"Brother Acolyte, sir." Lauren could tell the acolyte was back to his original imperious self, so she addressed him formally. "Something's bothering me. Why did the knight protector run off when he could've attacked us?"

"She's right." Aiden picked up the horn's damaged strap and showed it to the acolyte. "The way that knife sliced through this, he had to be aiming for it. Why did he go for the horn and not one of us?"

"He's unpredictable. Dangerous. Evil." The acolyte sighed. "We need to get back. It's getting late. We could be caught out after sundown, in which case we wouldn't see what else the Darkness might be hiding."

The acolyte's comment reminded Lauren of the brilliant light of Ethan's shield and how he said in his dream that it cut through the Darkness. Maybe it would be better to have their weapons if they were hunting the source of the darkness in the water. Lauren looked the boys in the eyes and shook her head from left to right. "Brother Acolyte has a point. We should go home., Only 'properly armed' warriors should do something so dangerous."

Aiden raised his eyebrows and opened his mouth for a moment to show that he understood what Lauren was really saying.

"Yeah, Mr. Acolyte, Lauren is right. Only 'properly armed' warriors should go after him." Aiden gave Ethan a big wink.

Ethan cocked his head and squinted his eyes.

Lauren wasn't sure Ethan got their subtle message, but she could talk to them later when Brother Flower wasn't around.

After what seemed like forever, Ethan said, "What weapon would Brother Flower use to get the Darkness?"

"Me? Armed?" The Acolyte took a step back, seemingly stunned by the question. "You're right. Properly armed warriors could go after the knight protector. But I'm no warrior. I don't know what I was thinking, leading you here, carrying a big stick."

He put his face in his hands and shook his head. "I was so foolish; I have no business chasing down crazy knight protectors or the source of the Darkness. The bishop will come tomorrow; he'll know what to do." He turned toward home, then looked back at the children with a grim expression.

Lauren shook her head in resignation, then slogged after the acolyte and motioned her brothers to do the same. As they walked, they saw that the stream was clear all the way home.

By the time they got back home, the sun had begun to dip down the western sky. The children begrudgingly agreed that the acolyte had been right in making them return home. As usual, on Sunday evening, they checked on the animals and retired to the kitchen for their evening meal of oatmeal.

They got no complaints about the food from the acolyte this time.

***

"Where should I sleep?" the acolyte asked after Lauren read out of the Great Book.

"The barn has plenty of hay in the loft," she said.

"You really want me to sleep in the barn?" The acolyte's face fell as if she had offended him.

108

"That's not fair, Lauren," Ethan said. "Brother Flower saved Sparkle Frog. Why should he sleep in the barn?"

"I'm not trying to be mean," Lauren said. "The barn is closer to the Tower of Light than the house. If the knight protector or some other dark force shows up, you'll hear them." Lauren pointed to the acolyte's horn. "If there's real trouble, blow that. The loft is high up, so the horn should be heard all over the Heathlands."

The acolyte nodded enthusiastically, and she thought she must have impressed him with her logic.

Lauren pulled a quilt from the back of her father's chair and handed it to the acolyte. "Here's a blanket. You probably won't need it, but just in case. You can find a sack of grain out there to use for a pillow."

"Goodnight, children." The acolyte thanked Lauren for the quilt. "Sleep well. I'll do my best to keep you safe."

Once the acolyte left the house and the boys were in their beds, Lauren sat next to them.

Aiden asked, "So the properly armed warriors you talked about are us, right?"

Lauren nodded.

Ethan asked, "What weapon is Brother Flower going to use?"

"Brother Flower's not coming with us. He was clear about not going after the Darkness. But I think Father was sending us a message."

"A message?" Aiden blurted out.

"Shh!" Lauren hissed. "We don't know who could be listening."

"What message?" Aiden asked, his voice a mere whisper.

"We have weapons made just for us." Lauren pointed under their beds, where they had hidden their weapons. "Father sent them to us for a reason, don't you think?" For emphasis, Lauren threw her hands up in the air. "I think we're meant to use them in this war against the Darkness." Lauren pointed at herself, then her brothers. "Remember the boy and the giant. He wasn't any older than I am. With God's help, he did what all the soldiers in the army couldn't do."

The boys nodded vehemently. Then Aiden scooted closer to his sister. "I believe God can help us, but how, Sissy? How do we fight the Darkness?"

Lauren looked out the window at the Tower of Light. "I'm not sure, but I think we can start with the poisonous sludge. It's probably related to the Darkness we saw on the way to church. If we can find the source, we might learn more about the Darkness and maybe even discover where Mother and Father are."

"That's a good idea, Sissy." Ethan scrambled out of bed. "Let's go!" He headed toward the loft ladder.

"Shh!" Lauren held her finger to her lips. "The acolyte was right about attempting things at night, so we'll go first thing in the morning before he even opens his eyes."

"That sounds like a plan, Sissy," Aiden said. "We'll leave him a note saying we went to get berries for breakfast or something like that."

Ethan smiled mischievously. "Yeah, and we'll tell him to start doing the chores."

Aiden snickered, and Lauren cracked a smile, then looked out the window. Her smile quickly faded as it seemed like the light from the tower had dimmed ever so slightly after the wisecracks. She shook her head and looked back out the window. It still seemed very bright, so maybe she was just tired.

"Sissy, what is it?" Aiden asked.

"Nothing," Lauren replied. "You boys, go off to bed."

The boys immediately jumped under the covers. After praying with them, Lauren took her time brushing her hair before bed. She couldn't shake the feeling they may have dimmed the Light with their mean words and intentions toward the Acolyte. She tossed and turned for what seemed like hours until sleep finally came.

11. Finding the Source

First thing in the morning, Lauren awoke to a sudden warmth on her face. She had been dreaming about wandering through deep darkness, but Meow-Meow had decided to cuddle up right next to her face. He was so close that she had to move just to catch a breath.

She turned her head to breathe and caught a glimpse out the window, noticing that the sky had just started to lighten. She considered trying to get back into the dream but realized they had to leave for their mission right away if they were going to avoid scrutiny from the acolyte.

Lauren gave the kitten a quick kiss, thanking him for his impeccable timing. The kitten appeared to be oblivious as he snuggled closer, purring. Lauren slid out of bed so as not to disturb him, threw on her boots and work dress, then roused the boys, who dressed just as quickly and grabbed their weapons. When all were ready, Lauren gathered up her spear and quietly climbed down the ladder, the boys following.

In the kitchen, Aiden started a fire, and Ethan got the slate and some chalk so Lauren could write a note:

THANK YOU FOR HELPING US.
WE WENT TO PICK BERRIES AS A SPECIAL
TREAT FOR YOU. PLEASE WATER AND FEED
THE ANIMALS WHILE WE ARE GONE.
WE WILL BE BACK SOON.

As she dotted the period, she could sense the light from the tower dimming. *They "were" going to get berries, so it wasn't a lie, was it? Should they really be doing this?*

"C'mon, Sissy, we need to make sure Sparkle Frog can't be hurt by the dark water," Ethan said as he tugged on her dress.

Lauren looked down at her brother. His earnest look convinced her to stay the course. *But would God really help them when they needed it if they were lying?*

Lauren wiped the slate clean, and the light grew slightly brighter.

"Sissy? Why did you do that?" Aiden asked.

Lauren took a deep breath and slowly let it out. "We can't start a mission for the Light under the cloud of a lie."

"Oh!" Aiden replied.

"You're so smart, Sissy!" Ethan said and gave her a hug.

"But what are we going to tell him?" Aiden asked with his arms outstretched and hands wide open.

"Nothing for now," Lauren said as she set the slate on the table. "Brother Flower didn't say anything about *US* going after the Darkness. He said properly armed warriors could do it, and I believe that's what we are."

She picked up the shaft of her spear in both hands for emphasis.

"Yay, Sissy!" Ethan said, holding up his shield with both hands.

Aiden lifted his sword in one hand and pointed out the window. "I'm ready to get the Darkness!"

"Shh, now," Lauren whispered. She was glad they were excited to go to battle. "We don't want to wake the Acolyte when we go out."

The children quietly left the house and hurried to the path that led to the stream, hoping the acolyte would not see them before they made it to the woods.

As they walked along the stream, they could see the tower's light whenever they reached a clearing. It didn't take long for the children to reach the pipes they'd plugged the day before.

The plug they'd jerry-rigged was still in place; only a trickle of ooze escaped from the pipe mouth and at some pipe junctions, but the ground acted as a sponge to soak up the leaks.

Aiden pointed his sword at the pipe that extended up the hill. "Let's follow this. I hope it stays above ground as long as possible. If we're lucky, it will lead us all the way to its source."

"Do you think the knight protector will be there?" Ethan asked timidly. Lauren turned to see he had taken a knee and was hiding behind his shield.

"Are you up for this, Ethan?" Lauren asked. She realized that for all of his bravado at the house, now that the danger might be very real, he was just a little boy.

Aiden must have seen it, too, as he knelt next to Ethan and put a hand on his shoulder. "You hold the Darkness back with your shield, and I'll get them with my sword, OK?"

"OK, Aiden." Ethan nodded from behind the shield, "We can do it together." Ethan stood up, and with Aiden behind him, they followed Lauren up the hill.

As Lauren led them over the crest of the hill, she saw that the pipe had been buried under freshly packed dirt. They followed the dirt mound through dense underbrush for about the distance from their house to the stream. When they came to the edge of the brush, Lauren could see a pillar of black smoke in the sky from a break in the brush above her. *This was it. It had to be the source of the Darkness. Were they really ready to do this?* She grabbed her spear in both hands and held it waist-high, a motion that blocked the boys from proceeding.

The boys stopped short and made eye contact with their sister. Lauren whispered, "Boys, we need to get low and stay hidden; there's darkness ahead." She took the spear in her right hand, about-faced, then knelt and slowly crept to the edge of the underbrush. The boys followed her lead, trying to remain hidden from view. Lauren suddenly peeked out from the brush.

About ten feet in front of them stood the corner of a big rough-cut log barn. The fresh dirt path for the pipe gently curved around the barn and to the base of a windmill. It looked identical to theirs at home, except this one had a squat shed located below the reservoir. The shed was wrapped tightly in a tar-soaked tarp, and a poorly fitted tin flue came out of the top of the shed. It leaked inky black smoke at its joints, and the tin darkened by the smoke.

The flue continued up to a height above the reservoir, and then the pipe narrowed significantly and turned into a *U* shape that went back down to a tube fitted to it at a right angle, which then dumped its contents into the reservoir. Above the tank, a haze floated skyward in inky puffs that slowly spread out, darkening the sky over the entire farmstead. Yet Lauren could hear no crackling fire, and she smelled no wood smoke. Odd. She realized they were at the parson's house. *The forces of Darkness have turned the windmill Father made into an abomination!*

Lauren motioned the boys closer. "This is the parson's house," she whispered. "He's the only one around with a windmill. I didn't realize we could get here by a shortcut through the woods since we usually come here straight from church."

Aiden pointed to the windmill. "That's horrible! Why is the spreading the Darkness?"

Ethan frowned. "I don't think it's him. Remember, he's missing, like Mama and Daddy. I think the Dark One caught him and is making him do this."

Lauren thought about this possibility. *Could the Darkness have turned the parson to evil?*

Aiden slowly unsheathed his sword. "Either way, we need to break that Darkness machine. If the parson's trapped in there, we'll get him out."

"Hold on!" Lauren turned toward Aiden and held up her spear in both hands to block his passage. "We need a plan. We should wait and watch for a bit to see what's really going on here."

"OK, Sissy," the boys agreed, and they all began to watch the farmstead grounds to see what was going on.

***

After what felt like the longest half an hour of Aiden's life, an unexpected "quack" came from the far side of the windmill.

Aiden jumped at the sound. Then a wave of dread came over him as he realized his favorite duck was landing in the

116

middle of the smoke. A growing fire burned in his chest, and he knew he had to join their feathered friend.

With Lauren distracted by Daddy Duck, this was his chance! He darted under Lauren's spear and dashed toward the windmill. As he neared the base of it, the fire in his heart seemed to travel down his arm, and real blue-white flames engulfed his sword. He was afraid of the fiery sword for a second and almost dropped it. However, the powerful feeling of righteousness in his heart steeled his resolve, and he plunged forward, flaming sword in hand.

Daddy Duck flapped his wings, took flight, then bobbed in the air on the far side of the windmill. Aiden joined him there and waved his sword, trying to shoo Daddy Duck away, but the duck continued to hover in that spot.

Though Aiden heard Lauren hissing for him to come back, he ignored her and went to investigate the shed, which seemed to be the source of the black smoke. He found a door with two iron hinges on the left and a locked iron padlock on the right.

Power welled up in Aiden, and it filled him with dread for what was behind that door. *Whatever it was, it was evil, and it must be destroyed. He had to open that door!*

With a downward swipe of his flaming sword, he cut off the door hinges, then switched direction like a master swordsman and sliced clean through the lock and hasp. He ended the second stroke with an overhead sweep of the sword and a turn. Now he stood to the right of the shed, facing away from it. He couldn't believe how smoothly and perfectly he moved with the flaming sword in his hand.

The air pressure of the smoke inside the shed pushed the door outward at the top, and it fell, landing with a loud crash next to Aiden's foot. He jumped back away from the fallen door and peered into the shed.

A thick cloud of foul black smoke billowed out of it, and he caught a whiff of the sickly sweet aroma. *Disgusting! It smells like dead animals baked in rotten fruit.* The smell was so bad he almost retched.

The initial burst of smoke rose quickly, taking the worst of the smell with it. As the air cleared, it revealed a black sphere, about half the size of Aiden, with three long spiked protrusions that kept the orb from touching the ground. Cracks in the sphere allowed a flickering crimson glow to escape from inside. Aiden stepped close for a better look. There was a kind of hissing noise like when steam escaped from the spider pot, and curls of the blackest smoke he had ever seen spiraled out of it.

Aiden stepped back, away from the shed and to his right, to see if Lauren and Ethan might be coming to help. He was worried about them since their weapons didn't look like they had power.

Above him, Aiden saw the flash that so often accompanies Daddy Duck's appearance. But this time, it was so much more. A ray of pure white Light shot all the way from the Tower of Light to connect with the white feathers on Daddy Duck's head. The beam angled off and shot toward the black sphere.

For a moment, it seemed like there was a swirling battle between the light and the smoke coming from the pot. The hissing sound reached a crescendo, and then the orb exploded into nothingness, taking the shed with it.

The blast wave knocked Aiden off his feet. He tumbled into the thick grass and rolled, hitting his shoulder hard on the packed earth, which caused him to drop his sword. He used the momentum of the fall to keep the tumble going and ended up back on his feet in time to see the windmill rock and then stabilize.

With the shed gone, Aiden heard the shearing of metal as the pipes tore apart under their own weight. Vile black water poured on the ground, smelling of decay. This time Aiden did retch.

Daddy Duck was thrown higher into the air, but he quickly righted and turned to fly toward home. When he flapped his wings, though they were small, they seemed to dissipate the dark haze that remained in the air.

Aiden choked back his revulsion, scrambled to his feet, and reclaimed his sword. Its flame had died out and didn't return when he picked it up. *Does that mean the danger is over?*

The sword felt heavy in his hand since his shoulder hurt from the fall, so he sheathed it and sprinted back to the thick stand of bushes where Lauren and Ethan were hiding. As he got closer, he saw his siblings staring open-mouthed at the devastation behind him.

He dove in next to them. "Let's get out of here," Aiden panted. "I don't have power anymore."

Lauren narrowed her eyes at Aiden as if she were about to say, *don't run off like that again.*

"Look!" Though he whispered, urgency swelled in Ethan's voice. "On the porch! It's the knight protector!"

The children stayed behind the bushes but peeked through a gap in its branches.

The knight protector walked out of the parson's house and stood on the porch behind the hitching post. He seemed to be looking directly at them. As the knight continued to look in their direction, he yanked his sword from its scabbard on his back and pointed it toward them. Then he reached out his hand in a gesture, motioning the children to come to him. Aiden realized that the Acolyte must be right. *This guy is crazy if he thinks we'll just come to him. He's watching over a Darkness machine! But I don't have the power anymore. We have to get out of here!*

Glancing at his siblings, Aiden shouted, "Run!" Then he tore down the path toward the stream. The others sprinted after him. When they reached the stream, they slowed to a walk, striving to catch their breath.

"Sissy, Aiden!" Ethan called between gulps of air. "We have weapons. Why did we run? We left the parson and his wife without any help."

Lauren took a deep breath. "The knight has been there since last night. If he wanted to hurt them, he already has. That's the only explanation for the darkness coming from their farm."

Aiden interjected, "E, we don't know what's going on, but he pointed directly at us. He wanted us to see him there. I think he's behind everything, and he's proud of it."

"So?" Ethan's eyes had a flinty look. "Aiden, you could defeat him! Didn't you see what your sword did? That was awesome! How did you do it?"

"I just felt the power come over me," Aiden said slowly as he tried to remember exactly what had happened. It went so fast he could only really remember bits and pieces. "I felt like I had to destroy what was in the shed, that it was pure evil, and it had to be destroyed."

"Well, the knight protector is a bad guy. Why didn't you just get him, too?" Ethan asked earnestly.

"I'm not so sure we could defeat the knight protector." Aiden pulled out his sword and showed it to Ethan. "See? It's just metal now. It stopped flaming as soon as the shed was destroyed."

"Strange. I didn't feel anything in my spear." Lauren looked her own weapon over for clues to what had just happened. "Ethan, did you feel power in your shield?"

"No. I didn't feel tingly," Ethan commented as he looked his shield over.

"Then I don't think we were supposed to fight the knight protector." Lauren's usual calm tone had returned. "The Good Book has a lot of places where it says, 'and the spirit of the Lord came upon someone,' and then they do something amazing. But then they go back to being ordinary after."

"Oh, I guess you're right, Sissy," Ethan said with a frown.

Lauren turned to Aiden. "At first, I was really angry that you went running off without us." Aiden could tell, by the careful way she was talking, she was trying hard not to lay into him with her mother voice. "But now that you explained it, I understand. You had to do it."

"Yeah, that's exactly how I felt. I had to." Aiden sheathed his sword but kept his hand on the pommel. He rubbed his index finger across the vine pattern in the crossguard as he talked. "You couldn't see, but the blade sliced through that lock and hinges like they were paper. I didn't expect that, nor what happened with Daddy Duck and the Tower of Light, either. He usually makes a flash when he comes around, but that was a big flash."

Lauren shrugged. "I can't argue with the results."

"When I saw the knight protector, I knew I didn't have any power. I was sure we shouldn't fight him."

Lauren nodded. "I don't know what to think about the knight protector, but that smoke machine was definitely something from the Dark One."

"I think it's connected to us, too. The Dark One broke our windmill, so we'd have to get water from the stream." Aiden shook his head in disgust, remembering the sickly rotting smell of the smoke. "Then he polluted the stream, so we'd either drink it and get sick or go thirsty."

Ethan patted Aiden on the back. "That's good thinking, Aiden. You're smart."

"Thanks, E. I can't imagine what else the Dark One will do to put out the Light. We'll have to be on guard until Mama gets home." Aiden put his hand on the pommel of his sword.

"We'd better get a move on," Lauren said. "Since Mama didn't come home with Daddy yesterday, I wonder what the bishop will do." Lauren leaned her spear over one shoulder and started toward home.

Halfway home, Lauren said, "We've been gone a couple of hours, but it's still early. I wonder if Brother Flower is even up."

Aiden nodded in agreement as the three of them picked their way along the side of the stream. He was glad they destroyed the smoke machine. However, he was concerned about how Acolyte would react to them actually going out to fight the Darkness.

12. Father's Instructions

On their way back home, the children crossed the little stream by their house and spotted a meager bush of blackberries dwarfed by a bigger one. Ethan had already picked a dozen before realizing he didn't have a basket and was trying to carry his shield as well. Finally, he set the berries down and put his shield on his back like a backpack. Even with his hands free, Ethan had a tough time carrying the berries without squishing them.

Near the house, Lauren slowed them down—she didn't want the acolyte to see them with weapons. They smelled the cook fire, and as they closed in on the house, they saw the acolyte walking from the kitchen to the chicken coop.

When his back was turned, the three snuck into the kitchen and found that the acolyte had been busy that morning. He'd readied the fire, and there was a hint of oatmeal cooking mixed with the smell of burning wood.

Lauren and Aiden put their berries in a bowl on the table. As Ethan reached to do likewise, he realized he had blackberry jam in his palm since the berries had been smashed.

Ethan licked at the sticky sweet mess; blackberries were his favorite.

"Eww, gross, E," Lauren scolded. "Seriously, you need to wash your hands." This made Ethan lick his hands more earnestly. He didn't want to lose any of the sticky goodness to the rough lye soap.

"We need to get our weapons put away before the acolyte comes back," Aiden said.

"Aiden's right," Ethan replied, concerned about the acolyte trying to take their weapons away. He wiped his hands on his pants, leaving purple streaks, and unslung his shield.

"Ethan!" Lauren scolded in her sternest mother voice. "Do you have any idea how hard it is to get berry stains out of clothes?"

Before he could respond, the door creaked behind him. *Oh No!* Ethan thought. *We're going to get caught, anyway. I bet the acolyte will take away my shield. God, how can I fight the Darkness without it?*

In answer to his plea, a sudden bright light shone from the tower through the kitchen window. Ethan's shield began to vibrate in his hands. He stared as it changed shape. It became smaller and looked like a small silver bowl in his hands. The quick transformation caught him off guard, and he almost dropped it.

Aiden's sword and scabbard shrank to a child-sized dagger, and Lauren's staff suddenly sprouted strands of straw from one end, making it resemble a broom.

When the light faded, Ethan grabbed a handful of berries from the bowl on the table and put them in the small silver bowl that had been his shield. He turned to see the acolyte rubbing his eyes and blinking. It was clear to Ethan that he was having difficulty focusing.

"Does that happen very often?" the acolyte asked, then shook his head, rubbed his eyes one more time, and then set the egg basket he was carrying on the counter.

"You mean a bright flash from the tower?" Aiden asked as he stepped up and picked up a washcloth.

"Pretty much any time Daddy Duck's around, you might get a big flash. We're not sure why he's so shiny," Aiden explained as he moistened the cloth under the kitchen spigot and began to wipe off the eggs.

"Oh, I guess that makes sense," the acolyte responded. "By the way, where have you kids been?"

Ethan offered his small bowl of berries to the acolyte. "We picked some berries."

The acolyte accepted the bowl and then looked over Ethan's head to the table. "That doesn't look like many berries. Were you all really out looking, or were you fooling around, letting me do all the work?"

"It's late in the year for berries, so we had to work hard to find some." Lauren didn't seem to look him in the eye, and Ethan thought it was because she felt bad for deceiving the acolyte. To confirm his thought, he could see the light from the tower dim. *Oh, no! We hurt the light! We have to tell him about the tower!*

Before he could say anything, Lauren continued, "They're all for you. Thanks for doing the chores. You've been a big help." Ethan began to pull on Lauren's dress to get her attention.

"I haven't done everything yet." The acolyte mopped his brow. "The cow still needs to be milked; I really didn't know how to do that. Also, I wasn't sure how much feed to give the animals, so if you finish up, we—we'll share these." The acolyte stammered as if he were embarrassed by the children's generosity. He dumped the bowl of berries Ethan gave him with the rest and set the silver bowl on the table.

Finally, Lauren turned to Ethan, "Whatever it is, it can wait until later. We have chores to do."

Ethan was very frustrated by this. *We need to tell to make the Light bright.*

"But Sissy!" Ethan demanded

"We'll finish the chores!" Lauren commanded sternly. She picked up the silver bowl in her right hand while she held the broom in her left. "Aiden, now that we are home, you should put the knife Father gave you away with the other special things like this silver bowl."

"Put my *knife* away?" Aiden asked with a raised eyebrow.

"Yes, in the trunk. *Upstairs.*" Lauren waved the bowl in Aiden's direction so a reflection showed a light spot on his face. "We shouldn't leave this out."

"Oh yeah, the trunk," Aiden said as he hustled to follow Lauren into the great room. "E, can you help Brother Flower with the eggs?"

Ethan was very concerned about them not being fully honest with Brother Flower, but he could tell by the way his siblings were emphasizing certain words that they must be trying to talk in code. They did that sometimes, and he could never really follow them.

Since his shield didn't "pop" back into shape when Lauren touched it, God must have wanted it to stay hidden. If they were taking their things upstairs, that was probably a good idea. *We need to tell Brother Flower the whole truth when Sissy and Aiden get back.*

***

By the time Lauren and Aiden returned from putting their weapons away, the acolyte had managed to fry some eggs, and the oatmeal had cooked as well. The acolyte put them on the table with the berries.

Lauren smiled. "This is great, Brother Acolyte."

"Yeah, really good," agreed Aiden between bites.

"Mmm-mmm," Ethan mumbled through a mouthful. It seemed like their troubles might be over. They broke the Darkness machine, so Sparkle Frog was safe, the acolyte didn't suspect anything about their weapons, and now Ethan's belly was full—without him having to do any real chores. Today was a good day...except for the Light dimming. *We need to tell Brother Flower the whole truth now.*

As he got up to put his bowl in the sink, he said, "Hey, Sissy," but was cut off when he heard the sounds of a horse and rider approaching.

He dropped his bowl in the sink and then rushed to the door to see who it was, and the others followed. He was surprised to see the Acolyte of the Dandelion Order, who dismounted his steed and said, "Greetings, Brother Acolyte. I bring news from the bishop."

"Well met, brother." Brother Flower pushed past the children and clapped the acolyte's shoulder. "Please share."

"The bishop has been detained due to a disturbance at the parson's house." The dandelion acolyte put a stiff arm around Brother Flower's shoulder and led him away from the children as if to speak in secret. "His Holiness was informed this morning that the children's mother is still missing. The Mighty Mercenaries claim she never made it to their encampment at Clark's Ford. We have no reason to believe she will be returning." The dandelion acolyte kept his voice low, but Ethan tiptoed close enough to hear. "You are to prepare the children to travel with us on the morrow. They will be leaving for their grandparents' home."

Ethan exclaimed, "We're not going with you. Mama said that if there were trouble, the parson would come to get us."

The dandelion acolyte let out a deep harrumph and turned to look Ethan in the eye.

"Since little ears are going to hear anyway." The acolyte paused and smoothed out his robe, and took on an imperious posture. "You will each need to prepare a bag of clothes and personal effects." He talked to the older children as if Ethan weren't present. "If your parents should return, they will assume we've taken you to your grandparents, as they'd instructed."

Lauren threw her hands up in frustration. "That's not right! That's not what we were told." Anger thinned her voice. "Who are you to take us away from our home? If we leave, who will tend our farm and the Tower of Light?"

"Children, this matter has been decided. You saw your father's seal on the writ the bishop showed you at the church. He clearly made arrangements to have you taken to your grandparents under these circumstances." The Acolyte of the Dandelion Order gave them a haughty look. "Prepare yourselves. Now!" In an ingratiating way, he put his arm around Brother Flower's shoulder and cleared his throat. "Brother, we have additional matters to discuss. Come with me to the barn."

Dumbfounded, Ethan and his siblings stood rooted in place. So much had happened in the past few days, and now they were going to be forced to leave their home and the only life they knew.

As the acolytes walked to the barn, Ethan ran inside and collapsed on the great room rug, where he cried over all the losses the past few days had laid on him. His siblings joined him and wrapped their arms around him. Together they cried and cried until they were roused by what sounded like hammering. Could things get any worse? Was someone attacking the Tower of Light? Ethan ran to the door and peeked outside with Aiden and Lauren close behind.

With pry bars, it looked like the acolytes were trying to extract the nails on the boards that the knight protector had been seen putting up to block access to the Tower of Light.

After many grunts and knocks, they managed to remove both boards. The Acolyte of the Violet Order put the boards neatly back in the barn while the Acolyte of the Dandelion Order went to his horse and retrieved a bag, which he carried back to the tower. Continuing to work, he removed metal pieces from the pack and laid them down next to the Tower of Light's door.

Ethan cupped his hand over Aiden's ear and whispered, "What are they doing?"

"Shh," Aiden said. "I want to hear what they're saying."

Lauren nodded in agreement. Though they tried their best to eavesdrop, they couldn't discern what the two were saying to one another.

The violet acolyte returned from the barn with a hand drill and made multiple holes in the door and post. Next, the Acolyte of the Dandelion Order picked up the pieces of metal he had earlier placed on the ground. While the children kept watching, the violet acolyte went inside the tower.

"What do you think he's doing?" asked Aiden.

Lauren shrugged, but Ethan said, "I think he's putting on a lock."

Next, the violet acolyte emerged from the tower. The dandelion acolyte shut its door and locked it with a padlock the size of a grapefruit. He pulled two large, black metal keys and a folded, black cloth out of his bag. He placed one key on the folded material, which he then handed to the violet acolyte. Then the dandelion acolyte hung the second key from a cord around his neck. With a nod, the Acolyte of the Dandelion Order mounted his horse and galloped away.

The violet acolyte returned to the kitchen with a dark, worried look on his face. His expression was so intense it seemed like he was walking in a shadow. This sent a shiver up Ethan's spine, and he retreated into the great room and watched from a distance as the acolyte said, "This is all for your protection. The bishop is concerned that I alone cannot defend you against the powers of Darkness that may attack. We installed a padlock on the tower. That padlock has special powers. Many say it is powerful enough to lock the gates of hell. I will keep the key safe until the stewards arrive tomorrow."

"The stewards?" Lauren asked.

Ethan wasn't sure what that word meant, but it sounded as though more strangers were coming to their farm. He didn't like it one bit, but the acolyte's demeanor kept him from saying anything. He was really scaring Ethan.

The acolyte nodded. "They will oversee the farm. The lock will protect the tower from further vandalism, and the stewards will manage the farm until a permanent solution can be found."

"But we can protect the farm!" Aiden protested with his fists balled. "This is our home; you can't make us go." Emboldened by his brother's courage, Ethan stepped forward to finally tell the Acolyte about how Aiden destroyed the tower.

Lauren shook her head and laid a hand on Aiden's shoulder. "No, little brother. We are just children. He is right." Ethan was shocked by this. *The boy beat the giant with God's help, and they had weapons that could break the dark things. Why would Lauren give in so easily?*

A look of relief crossed the acolyte's face. "Listen to your sister, boys. She is in the right." He sighed deeply and paused for a moment, looking at each child. "Now, can you please go pack for a trip to your grandparents? The wagon will arrive first thing in the morning." With that, he walked back to the barn, still holding the black, folded cloth in his hands.

"Sissy, why did you just say yes?" Ethan pleaded as tears welled up again. "Aiden and Daddy Duck beat the dark machine. God helped him! He'll help us keep the Darkness away."

"I know that's true, Ethan," Lauren said as she knelt next to her little brother and hugged him. "But Daddy was wise. He wrote that letter that we should go to grandma's. If we don't obey, wouldn't that dim the Light?"

"Oh," Ethan said almost inaudibly. He hadn't thought about it that way. "But, Sissy, why would Daddy leave us special weapons?"

"Maybe to protect us on our journey," Lauren responded while getting back up and patting Ethan on his head. "Maybe to go, rescue Mama. I don't know. But I do know that not obeying would be wrong."

"E, Sissy's right," Aiden said solemnly. "I don't like it either. But we need to be helpers with a happy heart now to keep the Light in the tower strong."

Ethan sniffed up his tears and took in a deep breath. "OK, Sissy, what do we need to do?"

Lauren got out their slate, wiped it clean, and began writing up a list of things to do.

***

When the night fell, the Tower of Light appeared bright as the sunset. However, Ethan was still troubled that they hadn't told Brother Flower about their adventure to destroy the Darkness machine. Ethan watched from the porch as the violet acolyte climbed into the hayloft. The little boy just wasn't sure how to tell his guardian about their adventure. He decided to wait until the morning. However, as he watched Brother Flower take up a watch position in the barn, he felt he had to say something.

Ethan thought maybe he would take it better if they all read the Good Book and prayed first. So, he went to the barn entrance and called for the Acolyte to join them for their evening family time, but the older boy waved him off.

Didn't the violet acolyte realize that at times like these, it was important to hear the Good Book? It told of all kinds of things to help keep back the Darkness. Of all the strange things that had happened over the past few days, this struck Ethan as the most peculiar. *Why would a defender of the Light not take time to be encouraged by the Good Book?*

13. The Struggle for the Light

After reading from the Good Book, the children went to bed. Sometime around midnight, Meow-Meow settled down next to Lauren's face and startled her awake from a dreamless sleep. She was about to scold the kitten for waking her in the middle of the night when the sound of a distant thud drifted through their open loft window.

Lauren rose and went to the window. Though the noise grew in intensity, she saw nothing unusual outside.

She was about to lie back down when something made a banging noise, like metal on metal. She squinted and turned her head. The sound came from the Tower of Light. She blinked and rubbed the sleep out of her eyes to see more clearly, and then they went wide at the sight before her.

It was the knight protector, struggling with the Acolyte of the Violet Order on the top floor of the tower. As the two men grappled with each other, they edged near the tower's large, glassless window. Lauren's vantage point from the loft window allowed her to see both men from the waist up. With the tower's light illuminating them clearly, she could make out what looked to be a hatchet in one of the acolyte's hands and a hammer in his other. The knight protector didn't appear to be armed.

Lauren's heart pounded. The metal-on-metal sound was the acolyte's hammer hitting the knight's armor! Her muscles tensed. Should she wake the boys and lead them dashing out to help the acolyte? She ran a hand through her hair. She didn't want to call attention to themselves and warn the knight protector of their presence, but she had to do something!

She stood at the window, begging God to give her wisdom. Then she felt drawn to pick up the broom that had been her spear. As her hand wrapped around the middle of its shaft, an aqua-colored light flowed over her hand and up and down the shaft—as it had done when she'd picked up the spear for the first time. The radiance reached the top of the shaft, extended almost a forearm's length beyond the end of it, and culminated in a sharp spear point. Simultaneously, the straw making it a broom disappeared. Spear in hand, she glanced out the window once again.

The knight protector had gained an advantage on the violet acolyte and backed him into a corner. As Lauren watched in horror, he knocked the hammer from the acolyte's hand.

The acolyte cried out, then reached for his horn.

Lauren's lips tightened. She prayed, pulled back her arm, and froze. *Could she really throw the spear hard enough to hurt a man wearing armor?* Then she remembered Aiden's sword. If it could cut through hinges and locks, her spear should be able to stop the knight protector.

She hurled the spear with all her might and watched it fly through the air. Just as it reached the window of the tower, the knight protector stepped aside, which put the acolyte's head in the direct path of the spear.

The violet acolyte lifted his horn to his lips as if to sound it. The watery light of the spear touched his raised hand.

The blue glow around the spear instantaneously disappeared, and the rounded steel cap on the end of the spear shaft slammed into the acolyte's hand. It hit with so much force that it knocked the horn out of the acolyte's hand and caused it to slam into his forehead. With a whiplash motion, the acolyte's head banged against the corner post, and he fell as if unconscious ... or worse.

The knight protector stepped back into the space framed by the window, looked toward Lauren, and pointed two fingers at his eyes and then in Lauren's direction as if to say, "I'm watching you."

Lauren went cold. What if the knight protector were to come after them? She stood as if paralyzed for a moment, then roused herself and flew to her brothers' bed, yanking off the covers. "Boys wake up!" she cried. "Hurry! Hurry!" She rushed back to the window, all the while urging the boys to get up.

The knight protector dropped out of sight, below the edge of the tower's window, then stood and began walking down the stairs of the tower.

"Boys!" Lauren grabbed each of them by the arms and shook them. "You have to get up! We're in danger!"

Ethan sat up and rubbed his eyes. "What, Sissy?"

"Not now," Aiden groaned. "Still sleepy, Sissy!"

"Boys!" Lauren yelled. "The knight protector's near! Arm yourselves!"

The boys didn't stir. Lauren rushed back to the window.

The knight protector emerged from the tower, stopped at the door, holding it open, and began fiddling with the lock. From the distance of the window, Lauren couldn't tell what he was doing. As Lauren watched, the knight protector took a cord out of his pocket, from which hung a key, and put it around his neck like a necklace.

Lauren froze. Where had the knight protector gotten that key? Had he stolen it from the violet acolyte?

The knight protector ran to the edge of the forest, then stopped, looked back at Lauren, and repeated the creepy motion he'd used earlier, first pointing at his eyes, then at her.

Lauren trembled, desperate to understand what had just happened.

The boys leapt out of bed and dug frantically in their bags for their weapons.

"You can stop, boys." Lauren wiped the sweat off her face. "You can't imagine what's happened."

"What, Sissy?" both boys asked.

Lauren swallowed. She felt extreme guilt for knocking out the poor acolyte, hoping he wasn't hurt badly. He could be a jerk, but still, he seemed to be fighting for the Light, and she'd just knocked him out. "I-I don't exactly know what's going on," She finally managed to say, "but I just hurt Brother Flower with my spear." Despite trying to hide her feelings, she couldn't help biting her lower lip in worry.

"Oh, no!" shouted Aiden. "Let's go!"

Still barefoot and in their nightclothes, the children hustled down the ladder. As they unbolted the front door, Aiden asked, "Sissy, are you sure we don't need our weapons? What if he comes back?"

"He's not coming back, Aiden." Lauren had had time to compose herself. "He always seems to be doing something dark and creepy, and then he slinks off when confronted. First, he boarded up the tower. Then he polluted the stream.

Then we saw him at the parson's place, seemingly up to no good. Now he's invaded our tower." Her voice had an angry tone. "I don't know what his game is, but he never attacks us directly. As Brother Flower said, you can't really figure out what such a person is thinking." She hurried outside, calling out over her shoulder, "Come on. We've got to check on Brother Flower."

The boys followed their sister with caution, despite her assurances that the knight protector wasn't coming back. When they got to the tower, they saw that the lock was secured to the ring on the doorpost in such a way that it prevented the door from closing all the way unless the lock was turned on its side as the door was pulled into position.

Odd black-and-red symbols with the look of a foreign script had been etched in a spiral from one end of the lock to the other. The lock's face was so black it seemed to suck up the light. An ominous symbol adorned the very middle of the spiral. The red metal embellishment was a circle with a pentagram inside it, the edges of which touched the side of the ring. The points of the star were arrows pointing away from the center, and the center was the lock hole.

The children left the lock alone and climbed the stairs to the top level, where they found Brother Flower, dressed in his robes, lying unconscious on the floor.

A piece of inky black cloth stuck out from under his legs. His horn lay on the floor next to him, seemingly unscathed despite the hit by Lauren's spear. Her spear lay on the floor beside the acolyte's hatchet and the hammer the acolyte had taken from the barn.

In his unconscious state, the acolyte appeared peaceful; the dark expression from earlier had been erased.

"Sissy!" Anger swelled in Ethan's voice. "Did you really hit Brother Flower with your spear?"

"I wasn't aiming for him. I was trying to hit the knight protector, but he jumped out of the way at the last second."

"How can that be, Sissy?" Aiden's brow creased. "When the power came on me, I hit everything perfectly. Are you sure you had the power?"

Lauren nodded. "The spear glowed from its end with that blue-green light. I threw it, and it even seemed to speed up, but the knight protector moved at the very last second." Lauren's throat tightened. "Poor Brother Flower. He was just about to blow his horn when my spear slammed into his hand."

"Ouch!" Ethan exclaimed, rubbing his own hand in sympathy. "Look at that bump on his noggin. I bet he's going to have a head egg when he wakes up."

Lauren's face fell. "I just hope he does wake up. We need to help him, but I don't think we can carry him down the tower stairs on our own."

"Wake up. Brother Flower," Ethan demanded, gently shaking his shoulder. "Wake up!" he continued to say, using more force this time.

The acolyte didn't move.

"Anybody home?" Ethan pried open one of the acolyte's eyelids. There was still no response. "Is he dead?" Ethan asked, wide-eyed.

Lauren's breath caught in her throat. *Could Brother Flower really be dead?*

"No, he's breathing, but Sissy knocked him a good one." Aiden turned to the door. "I'll fetch water. Maybe a good splash in the face will do the trick."

Lauren let out a sigh of relief as she knelt beside Brother Flower. "Ethan, you get a blanket. I'll stay here in case he wakes up."

After the boys left, Lauren picked up her spear, which showed no sign of its previous power, just simple wood worked to an even finish, with steel caps on the ends. In the light of the tower, she noticed, for the first time, scripted letters etched into her weapon, beginning at the edge of the steel caps and spiraling from one end to the other. The script appeared ancient but differed from the writing on the lock.

Until now, she'd thought this was merely a decorative line around the handle. Now she saw letters, though she could not read them.

A sob escaped Lauren. The mystery of the letters suddenly made her miss her father so very much. Her sadness was interrupted by Ethan tromping back up the stairs, dragging his old baby blanket just as he'd done when he was little. He must've found it in the great room chest. Lauren realized she should have been more specific with Ethan about what to bring.

Meow-Meow rushed in behind Ethan, pawing at the blanket's frayed ends. The cat looked as comical as always. Lauren allowed a smile. It felt good.

"Here, Sissy." Beaming, Ethan handed the blanket to Lauren. "My blanket will make Brother Flower all better."

"This wasn't exactly what I had in mind." Lauren reluctantly took the blanket from Ethan. "Don't worry, though. It will keep at least part of him warm."

With the blanket in Lauren's hands, Meow-Meow had lost his toy, so he instead rubbed it against Lauren's legs. She bent over and patted him. "Good kitty."

Aiden joined his siblings, his bucket half full of water. He plunged his hand into the bucket and sprinkled water on the acolyte's head. When nothing happened except that he'd gotten Meow-Meow's attention, he asked, "Should I just dump it on him, Sissy?"

"I guess that's all we can do."

Water poured over the acolyte's head. He sputtered, then resumed his previous state of inertia.

"Do we need to watch him until he wakes up?" Aiden asked.

"I guess so," Lauren said. "We can't move him while he's like this, but we shouldn't leave him alone, either."

As the children settled in to keep guard, Meow-Meow climbed onto the acolyte's chest, nuzzled his chin with his nose, and licked water off his face.

Brother Flower's eyes fluttered open, and he gasped, then groaned.

Meow-Meow jumped off the acolyte and scampered down the stairs.

"Ohh! My head!" The acolyte struggled to open his eyes.

"Brother Flower, you're awake! I'm so glad!" Lauren exclaimed, letting out a sigh of relief. She had been worried that the Acolyte might never wake up.

"Where are we?" The acolyte's eyes widened, then closed. "Why is it so bright? Is it morning?" With shaking arms, he pushed himself back against the wall and tried to stand.

"We're in the Tower of Light. It's not morning." Lauren patted him on the shoulder awkwardly, trying to comfort him.

"Ohh, it hurts!" Brother Flower cupped his head in his hands and rocked slightly.

"I bet it does," Lauren soothed, then turned to her brothers. "Come on. Let's see if we can get him downstairs and into Mother and Father's bed." Lauren tried to support the acolyte by placing her hands under his arms.

With everyone helping, they got the acolyte to his feet. Once he was standing, he swooned, but with the children's support, he managed to right himself.

Lauren and Aiden steadied the acolyte and gave him a moment to get his bearings. Ethan gathered up the belongings scattered on the lower floor. As he did this, Lauren saw him open the black cloth that turned out to be a large sack. He put the hatchet, horn, hammer, and blanket in the bag, threw it over his shoulder, and then grabbed Lauren's spear staff.

Lauren and Aiden helped the acolyte down the stairs and into the yard carefully. Halfway across the yard, the acolyte again swooned. Ethan dropped his load to help steady the acolyte. He continued to help get Brother Flower into their parents' bedroom. Since the acolyte's robe was soaked after the dousing of water, they removed it, dressed him in one of Father's nightshirts, and laid him on the bed.

It was still dark outside, so Lauren told the boys there was nothing more to be done but to go back to sleep. The boys climbed the ladder with Aiden in front.

When Ethan reached the top ladder rung, he exclaimed, "Sissy, I left the sack and your staff in the yard."

Lauren was exasperated. *This was hard enough, wasn't it? I guess he'd been pretty helpful in the tower, so I should let it go.* "Go get it, but hurry back."

Ethan retrieved the sack. When he returned to the great room, he began to dig around in the bag.

"What are you doing?" Lauren asked, a bit dumbfounded by his new antics. She was exhausted, and the last thing she needed was Ethan acting like such a silly boy.

"Brother Flower needs a blankie. They make you feel better." Ethan said in the sweetest voice Lauren had heard in years. Regardless of what a jerk the acolyte had been, Ethan really did love him for saving Sparkle Frog.

He opened the sack and put his head in it. "Sissy, I can't see anything, can you?"

She came over and looked for herself. Lauren couldn't see anything inside, so she dragged the sack back to the door, intent on using the tower's light. Still, nothing could be seen at the bottom of the bag.

This was peculiar. Shouldn't the Light be able to show them the bottom of the bag? She reached into it and touched the soft material. Her skin tingled. She pulled her hand out and looked at it. Nothing odd about it. Then she reached in again. This time she felt the hard metal of the weapons, but she couldn't see them when she looked. Shaking her head, she turned the sack upside down and dumped it all out. The blanket seemed none the worse for wear. Ethan picked it up, took it to lay over Brother Flower, and then hurried off to bed.

Lauren stood there looking at the sack for a moment. She remembered that the dandelion acolyte had brought it with the key. What was the connection between the lock and this bag? What was he doing in the tower with the sack in the first place? It wasn't exactly a weapon.

The more she thought about it, the more disturbing the whole battle in the tower became. The tower was locked, with its key around the acolyte's neck. If he went up there to stop the knight protector, that means somehow the knight protector had gotten the key from him to unlock it in the first place. Had the acolyte fallen asleep at his post, and the knight had slipped the key free to do his evil deed? Maybe, but that still didn't explain the sack. What was it for? She needed answers that she wasn't going to get until the acolyte woke up or they managed to capture the knight protector. As Lauren often did when she was confused, she decided to sleep on it and see if she could get clarity in the light of day.

14. Laying the Trap

Early in the morning, a loud thunderclap woke the children with a start. As they cleared the sleep from their eyes, they heard the rain pounding against the windows, almost as heavily as it had fallen the day before Mother left.

They got up and checked on Brother Flower, who was still sleeping peacefully, despite a swollen red bump on his forehead. They left him in peace and began working together to make breakfast.

"Sissy, what took you and E so long to come to bed last night?" Aiden asked as he fed kindling to the coals left overnight.

Lauren measured cut oats into the spider pot. "Ethan brought in the sack Brother Flower had left in the tower. It was so dark in the bag that we couldn't see anything in it, even when we opened it in the direction of the tower."

"That's impossible," Aiden replied between deep breaths as he blew on the fire to stoke it up.

"That's what I thought, which got me thinking about the whole situation." Lauren poured water over the dry oatmeal. "It just didn't make sense. Why would he be up there in the tower with it in the first place?"

Aiden coughed, having breathed in wood smoke from his smoldering fire. He hated when he didn't time his breathing right. All the smoke in his face had him crying like a baby. He wiped the tears away on his shirt sleeve. "He'll wake up soon enough, and we can ask him."

"If he was up to no good, would he tell us the truth? I just wish we could catch the knight protector and force him to talk to us." Lauren's expression changed from wistful to determined as she put the lid on the spider pot.

"Yeah, Sissy." Ethan pounded his fist into the palm of his hand. "We need a trap!"

"That's a good idea, E," Aiden encouraged.

Lauren was taken aback by their boldness. "Even if we had a trap, how could we lure him near?"

"He came before." Speaking in a whisper, Aiden leaned over the table. "I think he's out there somewhere, watching us even now."

"Right now?" Lauren followed Aiden's lead and leaned in herself. "In the storm?"

"I have a feeling he's hunkered down somewhere close by," Aiden responded in hushed tones. Then he waved Ethan closer. "It's the perfect time to build a trap when he won't suspect it."

"What kind of trap?" Ethan's voice boomed with excitement.

Aiden looked out the window, expecting to see the knight protector peeking in to spy on them, then gave Ethan a hard stare and put his index finger to his lips. "I don't know for sure." His voice was a whisper. "Daddy used snares and deadfall traps to catch forest animals."

Lauren rested her chin on her hand, "I don't think that would work," she finally said. "A deadfall deep enough for a man would take a few days to dig, wouldn't it?"

Aiden frowned. He knew he could come up with something; he just needed to think. He used the pause in the conversation to stoke the fire some more and added a couple of small split logs. "You're probably right about a deadfall, plus it would be hard to lay a snare that he wouldn't see."

Ethan reached up and put both hands on Aiden's shoulder to pull him down to his level, then whispered, "Aiden, you could wave your arms and get him to come near the house. I could be waiting up on the roof and drop a rock and conk his wonkus."

Aiden thought about it for a minute. He appreciated Ethan's desire to help, but that wasn't the kind of trap he was thinking of. He had to pick his words carefully to not hurt Ethan's feelings. "That's not a bad idea, but that might actually kill him. Rocks are hard and pointy."

Lauren scratched the back of her head. "Going outside and waving our hands won't work. He only comes out when he thinks nobody is watching."

They all stood in silence as Aiden continued to tend the fire. Then he said, "The acolytes took the board off the tower, and he showed up the very next night. If we messed with the tower, that might get him back here."

Lauren perked up. "So, what then? Are you seriously considering dropping a rock on his head?"

Aiden let out a chuckle, and a smile formed on his lips as he thought about that possibility some more. He rearranged the wood in the fire to get the best burn and replied, "Daddy showed me lots of ways to make snares and traps. I know a way to catch him once we get him in the tower."

"Really?" Ethan blurted out, despite his earlier attempt at being secret.

Aiden didn't think that it really mattered, given the hammering of the rain. He could hardly hear himself think. He worked to position the coals and new wood, so things stayed hot when Lauren put the spider pot in the oven.

"It's hard to explain, and I don't know if it will work," Aiden said as he took a step back from the fire and washed his hands in the sink. He still smelled like smoke, but at least breakfast wouldn't taste like ashes now.

Lauren shrugged as she put the spider pot in the fireplace. "We might as well try. If you're going to do it, you'd better get to work, even though it's raining." Lauren raised her voice to top the sound of the driving rain, slapping the windows.

Ethan looked questioningly at Lauren. "Sissy, what about Brother Flower?"

"Good question." Lauren went to stand by Aiden. "Do you think you and Ethan can set this trap on your own?"

Aiden nodded. He wasn't sure he even needed Ethan's help. But with how enthusiastic his little brother was about the whole thing, he didn't want to crush his spirit by not letting him help.

"I don't know how long this storm will last, but we have to take care of the farm before we make the trap." Lauren walked to the door and took her wool cloak off its hook. "I'll milk Clarabelle. Aiden, you said we needed more firewood, so run quickly and get it. E, stay here. If Brother Flower wakes up, give him a drink or whatever he needs."

Lauren tied the hood on her cloak, then turned to face Ethan. "In the meantime, work on your letters." Then Lauren and Aiden hurried off to do their chores.

***

After doing his chores, Aiden returned to the house long enough to wolf down some oatmeal and then grab Ethan for help setting the trap. They ran out to the barn, shirtless and shoeless, enjoying the warm summer rain and the mud between their toes.

Under the hayloft, they found a long piece of rope. The boys also came across a sack of wheat, which even both of them working together couldn't lift. Aiden realized that to get a big enough sack of grain for his trap, they'd need to empty this one out a little bit at a time and fill an empty one in the tower. He searched and finally found two empty grain sacks in a seldom-used stall. "Stuff as much wheat in here as you can carry," Aiden told Ethan, handing him one of the bags. Then he started doing the same thing.

After the sacks were ready, Aiden looped the rope over his head and stuck his arm through it. With grunts and heaves, both boys trudged outside, grain sacks in hand, through the muddy yard and up to the top of the Tower of Light's spiral staircase.

"E, dump your grain into my sack. Then go get more." Aiden puffed out, short of breath from the long climb.

"OK, but what are *you* going to do? Filling sacks is hard work," Ethan complained as he caught his breath.

Aiden paused, taking more deep breaths. "I'll be fixing the trap. We need a full sack to knock him out." Then Aiden unwound the loop of rope while Ethan went back to the barn. *I sure hope he'll actually get the sacks of grain and not just fool around in the mud. There's no telling when the storm will break, and I wouldn't want the knight protector to catch us while we're doing this.*

149

The top of the Tower of Light had a square-shaped hole about the width of two grain-sacks that allowed light to pass all the way down to the floor. A wooden railing that came to Aiden's waist surrounded the hole, with a pole at each corner and another pole halfway in between. From the top, it was a straight shot to ground level. The light illuminated everything inside, including the stairs, so there was no need for torches.

Aiden took the rope off his shoulder and tied one end to the railing at the top of the tower. Then he dropped the rest of the coil of rope down the hole. As he walked down the stairs, he saw the old torches on either side of the door. They had used them when building the tower. Since they never used them anymore, the torches were covered with dust and cobwebs.

Ethan returned to the tower as Aiden took a torch from the wall. Aiden hated the way the cobwebs felt when they stuck to his hand. He swapped hands and wiped the dirty one on his wet pants. Then Aiden patted Ethan on the head as he passed, saying, "Good job. Keep it up."

Ethan smiled and began to sprint up the tower stairs with his heavy load. Aiden was glad his encouragement worked. However, after a half-dozen stairs, Ethan slowed dramatically under his burden. Aiden spent some time trying to gauge the optimal place to tie off the rope for the trigger of his trap. Meanwhile, Ethan dumped his load of wheat in the sack and ran back down the steps.

Aiden tied the rope to the torch with a sturdy knot just as Ethan ran back out the door. Aiden pushed the wooden door shut from the inside and set the torch loosely in the holder. This made the rope cross the path of the door when it opened.

Ethan came running back with another full sack. When he opened the door, the rope caught and popped the torch out of the holder.

Ethan jumped backward, avoiding the swinging torch but nearly dropping his sack. "Hey!" His face burned red with anger. "Were you trying to hit me with that thing?"

"Of course not. It's the trigger for the trap. Now we just need to connect the sack and try it out." Aiden closed the door, reset the torch in the holder, put the loose rope over his shoulder, and helped Ethan lug his sack of grain to the top.

Deciding the bags were heavy enough, Aiden carefully untied the rope and rearranged it, so the line looped over the rounded handrail. Then Aiden tied the rope's loose end to the partially filled sack they'd just brought up. After the knot was secured, he nudged the bag over the edge, making sure to keep tension on the rope. Once the bag hung in mid-air, he let go of the cord, which held up as he'd planned.

"OK, E." Aiden let out his breath. "Let's try it."

"It's going to be awesome!" Ethan patted Aiden on the back as they ran down the stairs.

At the bottom of the tower, they moved carefully behind the door and pulled it open. When the door connected to the rope, it caught and, with a bit of extra force, opened. The torch popped out, and the sack came flying down and hit the ground with a thud right in the middle of the tower floor.

"Perfect, Aiden," Ethan said admiringly.

Aiden had been counting seconds from the time he pushed the door to the time the rope hit the ground, and he'd just held up his third finger for three seconds. "The timing will be tricky, so we need a reason for him to stop here." He turned to Ethan. "Run back to the barn and get the whitewash. We'll paint a scary face. Right here." Aiden pointed to the wall opposite the door.

"Yeah! Something with teeth!" Ethan took off as if he were on fire.

Aiden carried the rest of the rope and partial sack of grain back to the top of the tower. He put the grain from the smaller bag into the bigger one and reworked the trap but left the large sack of grain on the floor upstairs. He wanted to make sure everything was just right before he fully set the trap.

When Ethan returned with whitewash, Aiden made a mental note of how far the door could open without triggering the trap. Then he hurried to reset the torch. He was glad it looked like they both could just barely squeeze through the gap without setting it off…but a grown-up couldn't

Aiden watched as Ethan took off the lid of the whitewash bucket. "E, where's a brush?" he asked.

"I couldn't find one, so I'll use my fingers." Ethan jammed his hand into the bucket, then made a large circle on the wall, adding two smaller circles for eyes, a jagged line of pointy teeth, and horns sticking off the head. "There." Stepping back, he admired his masterpiece. "Is that scary enough?"

"That'll work," Aiden said. It wasn't high art by any imagination, but it would catch someone's attention. If the knight protector paused for just a couple of seconds, it would work. "Put away the whitewash and go wash up. I'll get more grain and set the trap. Don't come back in here, OK?"

Ethan's forehead creased with concern. "After it's set, how will you get out?"

"If the door's cracked open, I can squeeze out without setting it off," Aiden explained confidently.

After Ethan left, Aiden made three more trips to the barn, filling the sack at the top of the tower. On his last trip, he stopped and reset the torch, then filled the large bag of grain until it was bulging and retied the rope. Hands stiff from all the work, he moved the large sack over the edge of the top floor.

When it hung three-fourths of the way over the edge, it moved on its own. Aiden thought he might have sprung the trap too soon, but it stopped and swung back and forth just like he had planned. He stood, brushed grain dust off his hands, picked up the empty sack, and started downstairs.

Remembering an important detail, he whirled about and returned to the top of the tower for what seemed to be the millionth time.

At the window, he reached out into the storm and got soaked while grabbing the open window shutters. He fought the wind until he was able to pull them shut, and he wedged the edge of an empty sack into the frame to make sure the shutters would stay closed even if there were a strong gust of wind.

Before inching out the door, Aiden gave the trap a final inspection. It looked like it could go off at any second: just how he wanted it. He pulled the door shut and ran back to the house, wondering if the driving rain would ever stop.

Before he burst in the door, Aiden saw a most pitiful sight: Meow-Meow, on the step to the kitchen, completely drenched from head to tail. "Meow," the tiny kitten cried in the saddest way.

Aiden scooped up the kitten and carried him inside, where Lauren was helping Ethan get dry by the fire.

"Here's another one to help dry off, Sissy." Aiden handed Meow-Meow to his sister.

"Ohh, he's so pitiful." Lauren looked into the cat's eyes and cooed. "You poor kitty. You're a mess."

"He may be a mess, but the plan isn't. We set the trap, and I think I figured out how to lure the knight protector in."

"Really? That's amazing." Lauren handed a towel to Aiden and then found a handcloth and began to dry off her kitten.

Aiden stepped up to the fireplace and enjoyed the warmth and the smell of wood-burning. He couldn't help but share his strategy with pride. "I closed one of the shutters. It shouldn't block much light, but it'll be enough to get his attention. The knight protector won't like it, and he'll want to investigate."

"Are you sure that's a good idea?" Lauren wore a concerned look. "The night Mama closed the shutters is the night Daddy went missing."

"Mother shut them all; I just shut one side," Aiden said. "This should be just enough to get his attention. If it doesn't work, I'll open it, but I think we're sure to catch him."

The boys continued telling Lauren all the details about the trap, even describing the scary face on the wall.

"You're just lucky you didn't get any whitewash on those pants," Lauren scolded as she shook a finger at Ethan. "I'm already going to be scrubbing for an afternoon to get those berry stains out."

"But we have to surprise him, Sissy, or the bag won't conk his wonkus!" Ethan pleaded by banging his own head with the heel of his right hand.

"I hope it works like you think," Lauren said skeptically while shaking her head.

"It *will* work," Aiden declared. "We must be alert. After he's knocked down, we'll tie him up. Then we can find out what's really going on."

"I hope you're right," Lauren said. "Go put on some dry pants and a shirt."

The boys hurried off to comply. When Aiden was done getting dressed, he checked on the acolyte, who was still fast asleep. He wondered which would happen first: would the acolyte wake up, or would they catch the knight protector? Either way, they would get some answers about the fight in the tower. But would the answer be the truth?

15.   The Acolyte Awakens

After dinner, Ethan took a plate of food and a big tin cup of water where the acolyte lay in their parents' room while Lauren and Aiden were busy cleaning the kitchen. At some point, Brother Flower must have roused and settled back in, snuggling like a baby with Ethan's blanket. Ethan nearly said, "Aw," like he did when he saw newborn kittens.

However, the huge bump on the acolyte's forehead wasn't cute. In fact, just looking at it made Ethan wince. Maybe he needed to be woken up. Surely, he must be getting hungry. Ethan waved the plate in front of the acolyte's face, hoping the smell would wake him. He got no response, so he put the plate down on the nightstand.

Then Ethan poked him in the arm, but the acolyte slept on. Ethan poked him again. Still, not even a little stir. This made Ethan more worried. He pulled on the acolyte's arm. When the acolyte still didn't move, Ethan climbed onto the bed and used both hands to shake the acolyte's shoulders. There was no response.

Now that he was up in the acolyte's face, Ethan saw that the bump was worse than he'd thought. Additionally, the acolyte's face was pale, and he had dark rings under his eyes. Ethan thought for a moment. How else could he try to wake the acolyte? He stood at the foot of the bed for some time, wondering what might help.

***

"Sissy! Sissy! I have an idea; I can wake up Brother Flower!" Ethan called from the great room while Lauren was cleaning the kitchen with Aiden.

Lauren and Aiden rushed into the Great Room, "What are you so excited about?"

Ethan's reply was cut short by a loud rapping at the exterior door of the great room. The storm was so intense they hadn't even noticed someone approach the house.

"Hold on. I'll check and see who it is." Lauren walked to the door, standing on her tiptoes to look through the window beside the door.

Aiden grabbed her arm. "It's getting late. Who would be out now in this storm? What if it's the knight protector?"

"He's kept his distance so far," Lauren spoke with a hopeful tone. "Maybe it's a message from the bishop." Lauren stepped toward the door and looked out of the window. There stood a short man whose face was completely hidden by the hood of a waterlogged, full-length cloak. She couldn't get a good look at the man's face, but it clearly wasn't the knight protector. "Let me get it." She slammed back the bolt and opened the door.

Behind the waterlogged man was his horse, also soaked to the bone. Wide-eyed, the horse pawed at the mud, looking miserable.

The man reached into his cloak and pulled out a round leather case. "Message for the Acolyte of the Violet Order," he declared in a formal tone.

Lauren didn't want another stranger in the house, so she held out her hand and said, "I'll take it."

"My instructions were to give it to the acolyte only," the man said sternly, pulling off his hood. The older man had an intense gaze.

Ethan came running from his parents' room to join his sister and Aiden at the door. "He's—"

Lauren stepped between Ethan and the stranger. "He's unavailable."

The man scowled. "In this weather? Surely you jest."

Lauren realized the messenger wouldn't just go away if he had been commanded to make a face-to-face delivery. She had to convince him to leave the message with her, despite his orders. Without thinking it through, Lauren stepped closer to the man and whispered, "The acolyte saw someone trying to break into the Tower of Light. He chased after the intruder." She not only saw, but she felt the light in the tower dim at her lie.

"Break into the tower!" the man blurted out, then cleared his throat. "And the acolyte is out after him?" As if thinking better of himself, he lowered the volume of his voice to match Lauren's. "Why, he's just a boy. Is he out of his mind?"

Before Lauren could correct their story, Aiden pushed in front of Lauren and faced the man. "We're not sure," he added conspiratorially. "He said something about blowing his horn if he needed help."

The light dimmed again, and Lauren knew they needed to do something different, or they were putting everyone at risk.

"Horn? What are you children talking about?" The man threw up his hands and rolled his eyes like he was losing patience with them.

Lauren shrugged. By feigning ignorance, she hoped to buy time without affecting the Light. "We're just children. We don't know what to tell you."

Those were two honest statements. Maybe she should have started with that. The Light didn't dim, but it also didn't return to its former brightness. She hoped she could get rid of him without more lies. "We can take the message if you want us to and give it to the acolyte for you."

"Very well." The old man sighed. "You are right, young girl; many things are happening right now that are beyond my understanding, much less that of you children." He held out the round weathered leather case as if offering it to Lauren.

When Lauren took the case, the man turned toward his horse, then shivered and looked back at Lauren. "This storm is horrible. I'm not entirely comfortable leaving without giving this directly to the acolyte, but if it is as you say, it's more important that I get news of a tower intruder back to the bishop."

"The bishop?" Lauren grabbed the man's soaked cloak before he could leave the porch. "Sir, do you know about the plan to move us to our grandparents'?"

The stranger about-faced. "No, child, I know of no such plan. I am merely a messenger. However, the bridge between here and the main road is out. If I don't hurry, the ford I took will be too deep to cross. It may be some time before someone can fetch you."

The stranger hurried to mount his horse and prodded it toward the path. Her insides knotted; Lauren watched him go. She'd gotten rid of the man, but at what cost? The Light was not as bright as it should be. Should she run after him and tell the truth? Before she could decide one way or the other, Ethan ran out into the rain.

"Ethan!" Lauren yelled. "What are you doing?"

"Don't lock me out, Sissy," Ethan called as he ran off toward the creek.

Lauren left the door cracked and watched her brother disappear down the path. Her doubts about lying to the messenger were quickly overshadowed by frustration with Ethan's impulsive behavior. She asked Aiden, "Do you know where he's going?"

Aiden shook his head. "I have no idea."

They stood on the porch as the rain slowed and the wind died down. A few moments later, the storm had abated to a mere sprinkle, and here came Ethan, jogging up the path. The sky had started to clear and show the purple hues of evening twilight. Ethan was lit from the side by the Light of the tower, but he was bent over, with his arms wrapped around something they couldn't see. When he made the final splash and hop onto the porch steps, Lauren could see that he was carrying Sparkle Frog.

"You can't bring that wet frog inside," Lauren said, wagging her finger.

"But Brother Flower needs help," Ethan insisted. "I didn't get a chance to tell you, Sissy, because that messenger came, but Brother Flower looks bad."

Lauren nodded. She'd checked on him earlier and felt the same way. Between accidentally knocking out their guardian and lying to the messenger, she was doubting her ability to keep the Light shining.

"But Brother Flower won't stay bad!" His eyes danced with hope. "Sparkle Frog can help him again!" Water poured off Ethan, making puddles all over the front porch.

Lauren put her hands on her hips. "What do you mean Sparkle Frog can help him again?"

"Remember when Brother Flower hit his noggin on the church door?" Ethan replied in a matter-of-fact way. "Sparkle Frog got rid of his head egg. He has another head egg, just like before. Sparkle Frog can fix it."

Lauren and Aiden traded incredulous looks at Ethan's logic. Then Lauren said, "Fine, on one condition. Afterward, that frog goes back outside where it belongs. Mother would be cross if you left a frog loose in here."

The children went inside. Ethan handed Sparkle Frog to Aiden while he dried himself off. Then he took Sparkle Frog into Mother's and Father's bedroom and gently laid the creature on the acolyte's head while Lauren and Aiden watched.

The bump on the acolyte's forehead grew smaller, then disappeared entirely. Once it was gone, a bit of color returned to the acolyte's face, and the dark lines under his eyes vanished, just as the bump had. Then Sparkle Frog jumped into Ethan's hands.

Lauren's hand flew to her cheek. "I know Sparkle Frog is touched by the Light, but his miracles always amaze me."

Aiden shook his head. "You took the words right outta my mouth, Sissy."

Ethan gently squeezed Brother Flower's shoulder and whispered, "Wake up!"

The acolyte stirred and opened an eye. He then sat up slowly and looked around, wide-eyed, like he was lost, finally managing a hoarse whisper, "Where am I?"

"You are in our parents' room," Lauren spoke gently, but her voice swelled with relief. "You have been sleeping a very long time."

"Who are you? Where are your parents?" asked Brother Flower, grave concern on his face.

Lauren felt as confused as the Acolyte sounded. *What was wrong with him?* "I'm Lauren, and these are my brothers, Aiden and Ethan. You came here to guard both the Tower of Light and us." Lauren spoke slowly, enunciating each word.

"Guard you?" replied the acolyte incredulously as he looked around the room. "From what?"

Lauren stepped back, caught completely off guard by his questions. "Do you really not remember?"

"No. I don't remember you or anything about this place." He continued looking around as if taking in his surroundings for the first time.

Lauren had heard of people losing their memory from a blow to the head. She hadn't just hurt the acolyte; she had caused him to lose his memory. Now she felt worse than ever.

Ethan stepped forward and blurted out, "Whoa, Sissy; you must have really—"

Lauren clapped her hand over his mouth. "Not now, Ethan." She gave him a look that meant "be quiet" and then took her hand away. She didn't want to shock the poor acolyte just as he seemed to start recovery. "Brother

162

Acolyte." Lauren continued to speak slowly. "What is the last thing you remember?"

"Why did you call me Brother Acolyte? The last thing I remember, I went from the orphanage to the school at Emoh'nomed." The acolyte paused for a moment, buried his face in his hands as if he were trying to think, then looked up. "They tested me to see if I could go to school. I finished the first day with the opportunity to stay for the second day of testing. Going to sleep in the school dormitory is the last thing I remember."

Again, the acolyte peered around the room and even craned his neck as if trying to see into the great room. "That's obviously not where I am now, so how did I get here?"

"You were in a fight last night with a crazy knight protector. You must have been walloped in the head." Lauren could not make eye contact; she never could when she didn't tell the whole truth. But she felt the Light dim behind her. *But if I tell him I hit him, how will he react?*

Aiden chimed in, "From what you told us before, you've been studying at Emoh'nomed for the past two years."

"Oh, my!" Brother Flower pushed himself up so he could sit straight against the headboard.

"Right now, you are in the Heathlands at the foot of the Tower of Light." Lauren sat on the bed next to him. "You were sent to our farm to protect us until our parents come back." She clenched her hands together, wanting, needing him to remember all the events that had happened in recent days. "In fact, we've just received a message for you from the bishop, who apparently is your boss. He's the one who sent you here with us." Lauren turned to Aiden. "Get the case, please."

When Aiden brought in the case, the acolyte broke its seal and pulled out the parchment. He unrolled it and attempted to read it but quickly set it down.

"You say I got hit in the head. I guess I'm still not healed completely." The acolyte rubbed his eyes. "Trying to read this makes my head swim. Could you read it for me?"

"Are you sure?" Lauren asked. "The messenger said it was from the bishop and for you alone."

"I'm not sure of anything, but if this message is from a bishop, it can't be so secret that you kids couldn't hear."

Lauren took hold of the parchment and read out loud,

"Brother Acolyte, I was very disappointed that you did not complete the task put before you as instructed. Based on the severity of the storm, I can only assume that the weather interfered with your duties. As an acolyte aspiring to a higher call, it is imperative that you execute your assignment as quickly and efficiently as possible."

"I cannot stress enough how important it is for you to prepare the tower for the Y'lohnu Censer. This sacred relic is far more powerful than the lantern currently in the tower. It is imperative that we replace the lantern with the censer after dark tonight. Once you have removed the lantern from the tower and brought it to the ground, put it in the protective bag provided to you. It is essential that you then stand at the base of the tower before blowing the horn."

Lauren felt like her heart had stopped, and her vision had blurred, but she gripped the document tighter and brought it closer to her eyes.

The censer's appearance will be a powerful event, and it would be best if you were on the ground when it occurs. Once it comes to you, immediately hang it in the tower and then lock the door. Completion of this task will finalize your induction into the Order of the Dandelion Robes.

Aiden's face paled. "Sissy, that doesn't sound good." His voice was a whisper.

"Daddy would never want the lantern removed. It spreads the Light." Ethan's eyes burned with an intensity Lauren had never seen before.

Despite Ethan's passion, she considered the message thoughtfully. She had seen how things they had said and done had dimmed the Light. *Did the censer shine the light differently? Could it be powerful enough to make up for their mistakes?*

"It doesn't sound right to me, either, but if the censer is more powerful than the lantern, maybe that's a good thing. You saw how close the Darkness got to the tower until you broke the smoke machine at the parson's house." Lauren froze. She had just leaked that they went after the Darkness on their own. The acolyte would be furious at their deception. Lauren looked down at the parchment still in her hands, waiting for a well-deserved rebuke.

"Lantern? Censer? I'm not even sure where I am. What does this all mean?" As he talked, Brother Flower kept shaking his head.

Lauren let out a sigh of relief. He was so confused; he didn't pick up on her slip. Maybe their secret was still safe.

"That blow to your noggin was surely awful, but I need to help you remember what has been happening here." Lauren got up and set the parchment on the nightstand. "When we met, you said you were an Acolyte of the Violet Order, working toward becoming an Acolyte of the Dandelion Order. You are on your way to becoming someone important in the clergy."

Aiden hurried out and brought back a family portrait he'd retrieved from the great room. "Our parents are missing, and the bishop who wrote this letter sent you here to help us protect the Tower of Light from the forces of darkness."

Brother Flower looked past Aiden at the picture and stared for a moment in concentration. "I'm sorry, I don't remember any of that."

Lauren closed her eyes and stepped back from Brother Flower. There had to be some way to help bring back the acolyte's memory. After a moment, her eyebrows arched. She said, "You were given a horn that the bishop said even the hounds of hell would respect, so it must be very powerful. Maybe if you held it, you'd remember." She turned to Ethan. "Where did you put the horn?"

Ethan dashed out, then returned with the horn and handed it to Brother Flower. "See? Here it is!"

Brother Flower held it in his hands but shook his head, obviously perplexed. "I don't seem to remember any of that. I do remember respecting the acolytes and the clergy and hoping they would allow me to become one of them." Brother Flower ran his hand over the horn's shiny surface. "It sounds like I did well, and they gave me a mission to test me."

166

Aiden pursed his lips and paused before speaking. "That could be. The lantern mentioned in the document is hanging in the tower. It keeps the Darkness at bay, but recently the Darkness has been spreading. Daddy left to help keep the Darkness from coming to the Heathlands."

Lauren nodded, a grim look on her face. "Now, in this letter, the bishop is ordering a new light be put in the tower. Brother Acolyte, you are the one who is supposed to do that." This justified the fight with the knight protector. If the acolyte was in the tower trying to follow these orders, he would have the sack with him.

But if the censer was more powerful, wouldn't it just outshine the lantern? Why put it in a bag? Something wasn't right. She was missing something. They needed to capture the knight protector to get the whole story.

16. Like a Moth to the Flame

Clack! Crash! Thud!

"Sissy!" Ethan grabbed Lauren's hand. "What was that?"

"I don't know." Lauren peered out the window in her parents' room but could only see the barn lit from one side by the Tower of Light.

"It's my trap!" Aiden raced to the door in the great room. "Quick! Let's go!"

"Aiden, wait!" Lauren hurried after Aiden, catching him by the arm at the great room door. Worry seized her, and she squeezed his arm so tightly that her knuckles went white.

"Ow, Sissy!" Aiden cried wide-eyed at his sister.

"Just wait!" Lauren demanded as she let go of his arm and returned to the acolyte. "You've been out all day, and I'm sure you are hungry."

"Yes, I'm famished."

She picked up the plate and set it on his lap.

"We've had a wily varmint getting into things here on the farm. We're going to see if we trapped it." Lauren took Ethan by the shoulder and ushered him out of their parent's room. "We'll let you eat in privacy while we check it out." Then she stepped out and closed the door behind her.

"Quick! Get the weapons," she hissed to keep the acolyte from hearing and then ran for the stairs to the loft. When they got there, they found all their weapons were back to their regular sizes. The shield and spear had both broken through the burlap bags they had been stored in when they expanded.

"Sissy! The knight protector must be a bad guy! Look!" Aiden whispered as he pointed to the broken bags. "Do you think they're displaying power to help us fight him?"

"That could be, but we don't know that it's the knight protector out there," Lauren said cautiously as she grabbed the shaft of her spear, which didn't take on any power when she picked it up. This worried her a bit, so she held it in both hands and tried to will it to have power. But that didn't do anything, either. She decided if she needed the holy energy, it would be there like Aiden was given at the Darkness machine.

Lauren grabbed her spear and had to think about how she was going to get down the ladder while holding onto her weapon. Meanwhile, Aiden strapped on his sword belt, and Ethan put his shield on his back. The boys rushed down the ladder. When they got to the bottom, Aiden looked up as if to say, "are you coming?"

She hissed, "Catch," and dropped her spear.

Aiden caught it and set it next to him. Then Lauren climbed down and retrieved her spear.

Lauren looked both boys in the eyes to make sure they were paying attention. "Let's go. Carefully."

"Sissy, are you sure?" Ethan asked with a quiver on his bottom lip.

"What's wrong?" she asked impatiently. They didn't have time to fool around. *If it was the knight protector, he could wake up at any minute after being knocked out by the trap.*

"What if we didn't conk his wonkus?" Ethan asked with a tremor in his voice. "He could attack us."

"E, my trap worked," Aiden said confidently, beating his chest with his right hand. "I know it. But we need to go quickly while he's still out."

Ethan pursed his lips and squeezed his fists tight. "OK. Let's go." Lauren could tell he was petrified, and he was trying to be brave.

"Just remember the boy and the giant," she whispered as they set out for the tower.

***

The acolyte devoured the meager meal on his plate and downed the cup of water in one gulp. Then he sat there for a moment, just letting everything settle. His vision had cleared, so he picked up the letter and reread it.

He couldn't believe he had an important part in fighting the Darkness, which he hated with a passion. The Darkness had come to his village, and he had seen the wasting disease not only take his father but have an old family friend under the influence of the Darkness slay his mother. After his mother died, he'd lived in fear for weeks until the church at Emoh'Nomed had taken him in. He hated the Darkness for the loss of his family. But he hated it more for making him feel small and afraid. If he could banish the Darkness with the censer, then he'd do it.

As he contemplated his assignment, he stared out the window and realized that the last bit of twilight was fading. The instructions were for after dark. It looked dark to him. He saw the sack on the floor, and the kids had left the horn on the bed, and it looked like the purple robe with the green cord and tassels hanging in the corner must be his.

He donned the robe, smoothed it out, and tied the green cord around his waist. He wasn't sure exactly what an

Acolyte of the Violet Order did, but if they fought the Darkness, he was glad to be one. He put the strap for the horn over his left shoulder crossways so it hung at his right hip, and picked up the sack. If he completed this mission, he'd be one step closer to avenging his parents, so there was no point in waiting. Now was the time to act.

***

The children found the knight protector in a crumpled heap. A broken sack of grain and a tangle of rope lay on top of him, grain spilling over his body and onto the surrounding floor.

Aiden knelt beside the knight protector. With a satisfied smile, happy the trap had worked, Aiden coiled up the rope, unsheathed the knight protector's short sword, and set it in a corner. Aiden also removed the old man's dagger and used it to slice off a short length of the rope. *Ropes come in handy to tie up the hands of intruders,* Aiden thought grimly.

"So, it *was* him we heard, making all the noise!" cried Ethan, who, with Lauren, joined his brother inside the ground level of the Tower of Light.

Lauren hefted the sack off the knight protector, trying not to spill any more grain.

"Help me, Ethan," Aiden ordered, and they rolled the knight protector onto his stomach, pulling his arms behind his back. Ethan held the knight's hands in place so Aiden could wrap the rope six times around the knight's wrists. Then Aiden tied the rope's loose ends in a double knot.

"What's going on here? You said you were trapping a varmint." Brother Flower's voice surprised Aiden. The children were so caught up in what they were doing they hadn't noticed the acolyte entering the tower.

"I'm sorry," Lauren replied while the boys finished tying up the knight protector. "You were in such bad shape; we didn't want to worry you. Besides, the knight protector is like a varmint. He causes unexpected trouble on the farm."

"Didn't want to worry me?" the acolyte asked accusingly. "Worry me about what? Is this the man who knocked me out?"

Aiden had finished the knot and now turned to see Lauren nod silently. He wasn't sure how the acolyte would respond to this.

The acolyte said nothing, but his gaze immediately riveted to the sword Aiden had set in the corner. With careful steps, as if he were mesmerized, Brother Flower stepped closer and closer to the weapon, finally taking it up by its pommel. The second he touched it, it seemed to fly into his hands. He turned over the blade so that it pointed upward.

The acolyte straightened. "Get out of the way! Now, boy!" His tone was ugly and terse.

Aiden backed away from the knight protector and stood up, placing his hand on the pommel of his own sword. "What are you doing, Brother Flower?"

"Don't call me that. I am an Acolyte of the Violet Order, bound to do my duty and put an end to this false protector once and for all." He gritted his teeth. "I'm not giving this minion of darkness another chance to hurt me or anyone else!" He raised his weapon, ready to strike.

"No!" Aiden cried as the deadly blade came down. From the corner of his eye, he saw Ethan curl up in a ball under his shield as Lauren reached to pick up her spear from where she'd set it against the wall.

Time seemed to slow as Aiden gripped his sword, and the fire welled up in his chest and down his arm. He finished his draw, and the blue-white flames engulfed the blade as the acolyte's sword descended, point first toward the knight's chest.

Aiden hit the flat of the acolyte's blade with the flat of his own and swept up and to the left. Aiden's blade slid up the side of the acolyte's weapon until the flames on Aiden's sword began to burn the acolyte, and he dropped the sword.

"What sorcery is this?" the acolyte yelled as he blew on his burnt fingers.

Blue-green liquid energy surrounded Lauren's staff, which she used to sweep the acolyte's legs out from under him.

He fell to his knees. "Why would you prevent me from destroying a minion of darkness...unless you are the Darkness yourselves?" the acolyte spat.

Ethan popped his head out from beneath his shield. "Killing is a trait of the Darkness. The Good Book says, 'Thou shalt not kill.'" The little boy got up and dusted himself off, and stood with his hands balled in fists on his hips.

"He's right. God gave us the power to defend this man." Gripping her spear in both hands, Lauren stepped between the acolyte and Ethan. "He is no longer a threat to us. He's unconscious and tied up." She pointed at the knight's bonds with her glowing spear.

173

"We need answers we can't get if he's dead." She pointed the tip of her spear back at the acolyte. "You're not the sheriff or a judge. You have no right to kill a defenseless man in cold blood like that. That's a sign of the Darkness."

The far-off look in the acolyte's eyes dimmed. "You are right. I'm ... I'm so afraid. Like I've told you, my mind's a blur. All I really know is the Darkness can't be allowed to spread any more than it already has. I don't want it to take me, too."

Aiden stepped next to Lauren in support, pointing his flaming sword at the youth. "If the knight protector had wanted you dead, he could have killed you earlier, here in the tower." His voice swelled with such intensity it echoed throughout the tower heights. The acolyte cowered away from the holy weapon.

Lauren set one end of her spear on the ground and put her free hand on Aiden's shoulder. Aiden relaxed and held his sword across his body while Lauren continued. "At that time, this man fought bare-handed even though he had a sword at his hip. You had a hammer and a hand ax. When you fell, he could have ended it all with his blade then."

Lauren took a knee and looked the acolyte in the eye. "But he didn't. That doesn't sound like a minion of darkness to me. The whole reason we trapped him is to get answers about the Light and the Darkness."

The acolyte bowed his head, his cheeks red with shame. The fire left Aiden's sword, and Lauren's spear became a mundane staff again. Ethan went and hugged the acolyte.

Aiden picked up the knight's charred short sword and threw it outside. "We have a plan. So far, it's worked.

When he wakes up, it will be the moment of truth. Will you help us?"

His shoulders still slumped; the acolyte got to his feet. "Do I have a choice?"

"You can go back to our parents' room and wait, I guess." Lauren pointed toward the house while shaking her head.

"Brother Flower, there's nothing solid to bind him to here in the tower." Aiden motioned around the space in the tower, making sure the acolyte could see there weren't any good places to anchor the knight. "It would be better to take him inside and tie him to the kitchen table. He won't be able to move that; even our strong Daddy needed help moving it."

The acolyte nodded his assent, but the flat look on his face told the children he wasn't complying willingly.

It took all four of them to force the dead weight of the knight protector into an upright position and move him out into the yard. Before they turned toward the house, Aiden glanced back toward the Tower of Light. "E, can you open the shutter? Since we caught him, it doesn't need to be closed."

Ethan nodded and left to comply with Aiden's request.

In fits and starts, the other three dragged the knight protector across the muddy yard.

Panting, Lauren said, "We're almost there. C'mon!" Her encouragement and a final heave got the knight protector over the front door threshold and into the kitchen.

Aiden and the acolyte leaned the knight protector against the kitchen counter. Lauren lit a taper from the hot coals in the fireplace and asked Aiden to stoke the fire.

Once they could see clearly, they dragged the knight protector to the kitchen table, propped him into a sitting position against a table leg, then wrapped the rope around his chest and arms.

"Now what?" Brother Flower surveyed the unconscious knight as Ethan joined them.

Lauren examined the knight protector, not seeing any serious injuries. "Let's wake him up."

"I could find Sparkle Frog," offered Ethan. "He woke up Brother Flower, remember?"

Lauren looked thoughtful, then stood straight. "I've got a better idea, Ethan. Help me find Meow-Meow." Ethan set his shield inside the doorway, and the two of them hurried outside while Aiden tended the fire, and the acolyte was left to his own thoughts.

***

The acolyte studied the knight protector, searching for any clues that he would recognize this man. A glint of metal caught his eye. When he looked closer, he saw a key hanging from a leather thong tied around the knight protector's neck.

Like a torrent, memory pictures rushed into the acolyte's mind. As an Acolyte of the Violet Order, he'd vowed to take care of this key. It was his mission, and these children would no longer stand in the way of that mission.

He glanced at Aiden, whose back was to him, as he added kindling to the fire. With Aiden occupied and Lauren and Ethan fetching something, the acolyte crouched next to the knight protector with his back to the fireplace, concealing what he was doing. Then he pulled the cord with the key from the knight protector's neck and put it around his own.

"Hey, Brother Flower, what are you doing?" Aiden asked while holding a split log.

The acolyte froze, and all the color drained from his face. Had he been caught? He didn't think the child could see what he was doing. Regardless, he was going to complete his mission, but he didn't want to run afoul of that fiery sword again. He stood up and turned to face Aiden. "I thought I heard him mumbling something, but I guess not."

"Oh," Aiden responded flatly. "Why don't you come and stoke up the fire? I'll watch the knight protector."

Not wanting to alert the boy to his intentions, the acolyte smiled disarmingly. "Sure, I'd be happy to." Then he went to tend the fire, looking for his opportunity to sneak out and complete his mission.

***

Lauren returned with Meow-Meow squirming in her hands. Aiden turned from his watch of the knight protector as she entered. "Why did you get Meow-Meow?"

"I figured out how Meow-Meow shines his Light," Lauren said as she squatted next to the knight protector. "He wakes people up." Then she held the kitten up with both hands near the knight protector's slumped face. The kitten tentatively patted the knight's nose with its paw once, twice, three times, then licked the old man's bulbous nose with his scratchy tongue.

The knight's eyelids fluttered open. It seemed as if he couldn't focus at first, then made eye contact with Lauren. "What's going on?"

"We'd like to ask you the same thing." Lauren set Meow-Meow down, and the kitten ran off to the great room as Ethan entered from there. He picked the kitten up and exclaimed, "Sissy! I found him!"

Lauren stood up and shook her head. "Not now, E. Meow-Meow already woke up the knight protector."

Ethan frowned. "Aww, man." He let the kitten go.

"Aiden," Lauren hissed, "sword."

Aiden smoothly unsheathed his blade and leveled it at the knight protector.

The knight protector chafed against his restraints. "Child, you have no idea what you're doing. Untie me now while the damage can be undone." He looked around wildly as if trying to find a way to escape his bonds. "I'm the only thing standing between you and your family's imminent destruction by the Dark One." He strained intensely against his bonds, to no avail. Lauren was impressed with how well Aiden had tied the knots. "You've got to listen to me!"

"You listen." Lauren pointed her spear at the knight protector. "We're asking the questions now."

Aiden nodded in agreement while holding his sword steady.

Emboldened by her brother's support, Lauren slammed the blunt end of her spear on the floor and demanded, "Why were you boarding up the Tower of Light?"

"To keep the forces of darkness from getting to the lantern." The knight exhaled and slumped back against the table leg. "At the time, I wasn't sure who they might send or how it would happen. By boarding up the lantern, I thought I could slow them enough to fight them off should they try a direct attack."

"That's a convenient answer." Lauren could tell from his body language that he was resigned to the questioning, so she squatted down to his level, still holding her spear in one hand. She wanted to get a better look at his face to see if he looked evasive or like he was lying.

Aiden stepped toward the knight, menacing with his sword. "If that's true, why were you polluting the river?"

"I wasn't." As if exasperated, the knight protector rolled his eyes. "I was loosening the pipes so I could redirect the sludge."

"Then why did you run away?" asked Lauren as she searched her memory of the event. Could he really have been breaking the sludge pipes? "Why didn't you just stop and tell us that?"

"There was no time. I couldn't risk the acolyte blowing his cursed horn." The knight protector's face reddened, and his voice got stern. "He's only a boy. Yes, he's studied for two years, but he doesn't understand what he's doing. I didn't want him hurt."

Lauren again banged the blunt end of her spear on the floor in frustration. "Then why were you fighting him in the tower?"

"Think about it, child. Why was he in the tower in the middle of the night?" The knight protector impatiently shook his head. "You children are in so far over your heads." He sighed. "I followed him to the top of the tower and caught him in the act of taking down the lantern. If you hadn't thrown your spear when you did, young lady, I'm sure he would have blown that blasted horn of his. There's no telling what evil would have descended upon us then."

"You keep talking about his horn like it's some horrible thing." Aiden bent over, so he was at eye level with the knight protector. "The bishop told us it was so powerful, even the hounds of hell would respect it."

"Is that how he described it?" The knight protector smirked. "Clever man, that bishop. Let me guess. He told you he was looking out for your good and that he would send people to watch over you."

Lauren and Aiden eyed each other, surprised the knight protector knew so much of their story.

Trying to keep his voice steady, the captive continued describing a different perspective on the events of the past days. "By offering to protect you with one of his own, the bishop gained direct access to this home. To the Tower of Light itself."

Lauren wobbled a bit, then straightened. "How ... how did you know?"

"Children, please release me. The reckoning hour is near. It's already past dark. I've no time to explain now." The knight protector again struggled against his binding. "You must free me before it's too late."

A horse whinnied. The children turned to see the acolyte rushing out the kitchen door. For an instant, Lauren was torn. *Was it Mother returning with Father, or was it the bishop's people coming to take them away?* Feeling the strength of Father's spear in her hand, she was ready for either, so she hurried after the acolyte, and the boys followed.

"Children, wait!" the knight protector cried. "That must be the other acolyte." Urgency shrilled his voice. "Again, I beg you, untie me before it's too late!"

As Lauren stepped off the porch onto the muddy yard, she stopped short in caution, holding her free hand out to slow Aiden, who was just behind her. The horse was not Mother returning but the Acolyte of the Dandelion Order. As the children approached, he dismounted his steed and joined the violet acolyte, who stood at the foot of the tower.

"Well met, Brother!" The Acolyte of the Dandelion Order clapped the violet acolyte on the back. "I heard you were chasing the knight protector. You didn't blow your horn for assistance. Were you able to capture him?"

The violet acolyte stared at the young man and paused for what seemed an eternity before he spoke, "He's tied up in the kitchen. Are you here because the bishop didn't believe I could finish the mission?"

"Honestly, yes." The dandelion acolyte patted the violet acolyte's back. "I, too, was a little worried, Brother, but I see I underestimated you."

"I will finish this now!" The Acolyte of the Violet Order patted the black sack where it was tucked in his belt and sprinted up the tower.

"Brother Flower!" Lauren yelled as he passed beyond view.

The dandelion acolyte stiffened, then turned to look at the children. "Why are you children awake ... and armed?" He stepped back, and his foot settled on the knight protector's short sword where Aiden had thrown it earlier. He looked down, squatted to pick it up, and brandished it toward them. "You'd best be off to bed, children."

The more the acolyte of the yellow robes spoke, the darker his expression became.

Blood drained from Lauren's face. "Brother Flower," she cried up to the acolyte who had reached the top of the tower, "Don't take the lantern down. Something's not right. Please stop!"

Lauren turned to Aiden, who stood beside her, with Ethan behind them. "I'm scared!" Ethan whimpered and turned, and sprinted toward the house.

"Please, God," Lauren whispered, crestfallen at Ethan's reaction. "Give us the power to overcome this new challenge. Please help!"

Ignoring Lauren's plea, the violet acolyte took the lantern off its hook, then glanced out the window. Without the lantern in place, Darkness filled the yard.

Lantern in hand, the violet acolyte ran to the bottom of the tower into the yard and stood by the dandelion acolyte. Light again illuminated the farm.

"Brother Flower!" Lauren cried. She and Aiden were only a few steps from the tower door. "Put the lantern back!" With the end of her spear, she pointed to the top of the tower.

The violet acolyte shook his head. "No, children. I must finish my task and replace it. The censer is much more powerful. It's time to put in place something that can really hold back the Darkness!"

Lauren and Aiden rushed toward the acolytes while Ethan ran inside the house.

"Don't come a step closer!" The dandelion acolyte leveled the knight protector's sword at the children. His eyes on the children, he said, "Brother, put the lantern in the protective case."

"Of course." The violet acolyte pulled the sack from his belt.

"No, Brother Flower! Don't cover up the Light! Don't let the Darkness overtake us!" Lauren gripped her spear, but its point did not emerge. Aiden's sword wasn't on fire. Why wasn't God giving them the power to defeat the Darkness?

"Brother, it will only be for a moment," the dandelion acolyte said. "Now is the time. Use the horn as you were instructed. The Y'lohnu Censer will appear and take over for the lantern." With a wave of the sword, the dandelion acolyte again threatened the children.

The violet acolyte stashed the lantern in the sack.

Utter blackness fell on the yard. The only light came from inside the house, escaping through the windowpane: it was the glow of the fire and the candles Lauren had lit. In the darkness, Lauren knew with certainty what she'd increasingly begun to suspect: letting the lantern come down was a huge mistake.

"Brother, please! Let the lantern shine!" Aiden cried. "Uncover it! This can't be right!"

Lauren could barely make out Aiden as he advanced on the acolytes in the near pitch-black night. She saw him grip his sword with both hands now, yet it failed to catch fire. *Why did it not ignite?* She tried willing power into her own weapon but to no avail. *God, why aren't you helping us?*

In the dim light, Lauren saw the violet acolyte put the horn to his lips, releasing a deep, echoing tone that rang across the Heathlands. A ring of fire erupted from the mouth of the horn, leapt into the air, and expanded until it was the size of the yard. Then it fell to the ground, leaving a burning ring of fire that filled the space between the house and the tower, with Lauren, Aiden, and the acolytes inside the ring and Ethan in the shadows on the porch, just outside. Lauren was terrified by the fire erupting all around her. Without the light of the lantern and no power from their weapons, how could they stand against whatever was coming next?

As the acolyte continued to blow the horn, lances of fire shot out of it. Each lance rocketed upward, then landed until the arcs of fire on the ground matched the same star pattern as was on the face of the lock on the Tower of Light's door frame. From each of the five points of the star in the symbol emerged black hounds the size of horses, with bodies covered in scales. Their heads looked more like those of wolves than dogs. Black spittle foamed on their teeth and dripped from their mouths. Puffs of black smoke escaped their nostrils. When all five were fully formed, they each let out a hellish howl. At this, Lauren cowered in fear. *Oh, God, please help us!*

In the center of the symbol, an immense ball of fire appeared in an explosion that knocked the children and the acolytes to the ground. From this fireball came thick black smoke. As the smoke rose, a black sphere, two feet in width, began to emerge. The censer! The orb rested on three spikes, like the one Aiden had destroyed at the parson's farm. The sphere spewed black, choking smoke skyward. Lauren hit her head as she was blown backward by the explosion. Her vision blurred from the concussion and smoke. All she could see was the flame and smoke surrounding her.

Gradually the air around the censer cleared.

In the center of the pentagram stood ... the bishop!

"Well done, young acolyte!" The bishop extended his hand and helped the violet acolyte stand. "You have earned your place among the brotherhood, doing what I could not. That lantern's direct light would have been the death of me. Now I'll take back the horn of power, thank you very much."

The bishop stepped to the Acolyte of the Violet Order and picked up the horn, then turned toward the children. Through her blurred vision and the haze of flame and smoke, Lauren saw the bishop's lips stretch into a hideous grin as he looked to where she and Aiden lay. "Ho-ho. Look! You've even been considerate enough to provide a few delectable morsels for the hounds."

The hounds let out another unearthly howl and stalked toward Lauren and Aiden. Her fear of the advancing beasts couldn't overcome the damage from the blow to her head as Lauren struggled to move but could not even keep her eyes open. None of her muscles obeyed. "Oh, God!" she whispered ... or was she only thinking the thought? Her lips didn't seem to be working, either. "Why didn't you give me the power to prevent this nightmare?" Then everything went black.

17.   Let it Shine

When Ethan ran away, he ducked behind the kitchen door to hide. He found his shield there, quickly put it on his back, and curled up under it like a turtle. Then darkness fell save for candlelight and firelight from the oven, the latter reflecting brightly off his shield. There was an explosion that caused Ethan to pull even tighter under his protective barrier.

"Shieldbearer!" yelled the knight protector, who strained so fiercely against his restraints, he managed to drag the table askew. "I have a message from your father!"

Ethan's throat tightened. Dare he go listen to the crazy man? His shield would keep him safe here. Still, if Daddy told this man something, it must be important. He poked his head out and asked: "OK, what did Daddy say?"

"Let your little light shine!"

Ethan bit his lip. Father *would* say such a thing. But what light? He got up on one knee, looked around, and caught candlelight wildly reflecting off his shield in a mirror by the door. He took it off his back and put it on his arm. He saw that he could direct where the reflections were going by where he pointed the shield.

What if the knight protector spoke the truth? Ethan stood up and went to the door, desperate to do what was right. Whom should he believe?

He looked out the front door, where it was pitch black except for the flaming ring of fire in front of him. That blaze weirdly didn't reflect off his shield. The fire ring in front of Ethan created a burning fence between him and his siblings. He stiffened. His heart thundered in his chest, and his hands shook. Red and orange tongues danced in front of him, heating his whole body so that he began to sweat.

"There's no light, just fire!" Ethan cried back to the knight protector.

"Shine YOUR light, boy!" the knight protector implored.

Even over the roar of fire and howling of hounds, he heard the bishop's awful laugh and saw his crazed face. He tried to think of what Father would do. It had been so long since Father's deep and steady voice explained things.

Outside, a victorious howl came from the throats of those hideous beasts. Ethan dove to the wooden decking of the porch and pulled the shield over him again. From this position, all he could see was Lauren and Aiden helplessly lying on the ground, about to be eaten by five hellhounds, their mouths chomping as they crept nearer to his brother and sister.

Fear rooted Ethan to the porch, but he managed a hoarse scream. The hounds became still as statues. Then their heads and necks swiveled as they sniffed the air.

Ethan's eyes widened. The Darkness was more awful than ever. Far, far worse now, with these horrid beasts!

Five sets of canine eyes stared straight at him. One of the terrible creatures licked its lips.

On the other side of the yard, the bishop thrust his hand in Ethan's direction. "One of you, make sure that boy doesn't get away." Ethan realized his head was sticking out of his turtle disguise, so he moved the shield up in front of him and crouched behind it. From behind the shield, he heard the bishop cackling. "Mayhem! Strife! Conflict! My good hounds! Finish these two as well."

Ethan peeked around the right side of the shield. He was horrified to see the two hounds closest to him turn and lope through the wall of fire as if they weren't there while the three on the other side of the yard stalked toward his siblings.

"Help!" Sobs caught in Ethan's throat. "Somebody help!"

"Shine your light, boy!" The grizzled voice of the knight protector rang out from inside the house. "Shine your light!"

"What light? What do you mean?" Ethan held his shield in front of him and slowly scooted backward until he smacked against the kitchen door frame. "What light?"

The pair of hounds skulked closer.

"I need my Daddy!" Ethan cried.

The narrow beam of light coming from the house allowed him to notice the engraving of the Lantern of Light on his shield. It began to glow ever so softly. A memory of Father rose from the present chaos …

They'd gathered around the kitchen table, on which had been set the lantern from the Tower of Light.

Father pointed at Ethan's chest. "The light for this lantern is inside of each of us."

Ethan looked down at his chest, then threw his hands in the air. "I don't see the light, Daddy."

"When you love the Lord with all your heart, mind, and soul, the Good Book says you reflect the Savior's Light on the world." Father patted Ethan's head. "Would you like to learn a song about how we can shine that light?"

Ethan stood up and stepped forward, away from the kitchen door. His memory echoed the same words the old knight protector had just yelled. With the Light, he could stand on his own. He could fight the Darkness. He had the Light. Of course! He'd had it all the time!

The hounds crept closer, closer.

"This little light of mine, I'm gonna let it shine." Ethan's lips quivered with fear, so he focused on the memory of his family gathered around the lantern's light. "This little light of mine, I'm gonna let it shine, let it shine, let it shine!" His voice swelled, and the lantern in the center of his shield glowed with intense, blue-white light.

Warmth engulfed Ethan. He *would* fight the Darkness. The Light would help! "Won't hide it under a bushel. NO! I'm gonna let it shine!" His voice rang loud and clear, cutting through the dark, chaotic night. Ethan's small buckler transformed into a tower shield big enough for his father, yet he could carry it with ease and even somehow see through it.

The pair of hounds stood still and eyed each other. One pawed the ground, sending mud clods flying.

"Won't let the Dark One blow it out." Buoyed by the Light's power, Ethan stepped off the porch, slammed the point of his shield into the ground, and braced himself for the hounds' attack. "I'm gonna let it shine!"

As if they were synchronized, the hounds leapt at Ethan. Snarls filled the air.

"Won't let the Dark One blow it out." Ethan tightened every muscle in his body, closed his eyes, and continued to sing, "I'm gonna let it shine."

The hounds rammed the shield, which erupted with a white-blue blaze that originated from the lantern emblem.

When Ethan didn't feel the hounds slam into him, he opened his eyes and did a double-take. The hounds were gone. A mist rose from the spot where they'd banged against the shield. They'd ... they'd been vaporized.

Ethan's chest swelled with hope. With the Light inside him, he could help his Sissy and Aiden, still seemingly unconscious inside the ring of fire. Fire rose up in Ethan, which seemed to burn hotter than the fire in front of him. Ethan advanced slowly toward his siblings, with the fire on the ground parting around the protective bubble of light surrounding Ethan and the shield.

Ethan saw the three remaining hounds, slowly but steadily, padding closer to his siblings.

"Bishop!" Brother Flower stepped into the light emanating from Ethan's shield. "What are you doing? Why would you want to kill innocent children?" His countenance pale, he pointed his sword at the bishop. "It was you all along, spreading the Darkness. You fooled me!"

"Who do you think you are to speak to me that way, boy?" retorted the bishop. "You'd best remember who you serve! What do you know of, right? Clearly, your studies have been incomplete." He grinned evilly. "There is nothing innocent about these children. They are bearers of the Light! They and their abominable Tower of Light are blocking the master's dominance of this land."

"I won't let you harm them!" Sword in hand, Brother Flower charged the bishop.

"Mayhem!" the bishop yelled.

The three hounds, who'd locked their eyes on Ethan's siblings, whirled around.

"Mayhem, attack!" yelled the bishop.

The largest of the three hounds crouched, then pounced in an arc that spanned the entire circle and slammed into Brother Flower. The acolyte managed to lift his sword as the beast fell on him. He lodged his weapon sideways into the beast's mouth. As man and beast fell to the ground, Mayhem's claws ripped open Brother Flower's chest.

Ethan saw the acolyte struggle to free his blade and cried, "No!" Then Ethan froze as he watched the combat unfold. *I hope Brother Flower will be OK. But Sissy and Aiden need me.*

Blood began to gush from the beast's wound, and the hound gave a strangled cry and backed away, shaking his head vigorously, desperate to rid himself of the blade.

"Well played, boy," the bishop cackled. "Few could foil a hound of hell." He shook his head in mock regret. "So much potential." Then his lips tightened, and he turned to the Acolyte of the Dandelion Order. "Finish him!" When the acolyte didn't budge, he shouted, "Hounds, now is the time. Kill the children!"

The bishop's harsh words and the sight of Brother Flower's grievous wounds emboldened Ethan to return to the fight. "Shine it over the whole wide world."

His courage to begin the song again came just in time, for the two remaining hounds turned around and bore down on his Sissy and brother. "Oh, God," Ethan whispered, "let them be OK." He squared his shoulders and resumed his forward advance toward the circle, singing in cadence with his steps. "This little light of mine, I'm gonna let it shine!" His lantern shield lit up the yard as if it were daylight.

The hounds of hell cringed as if the light hurt not only their eyes but their bodies. Even the Acolyte of the Dandelion Order shielded his eyes.

With every word Ethan sang, his stride grew. Holding his shield in front of him, he reached the edge of the circle of fire. The flames parted, making a path for Ethan and his little light.

"Strife! Conflict! Kill that boy first!" The bishop's voice had gone hoarse from all his screaming. The evil man knelt beside Mayhem, grunting and yanking, desperate to extract the blade from the hound's mouth.

Strife and Conflict moved toward Ethan, who planted his shield into the ground, facing them. "This little light," he kept singing, his voice ringing loud and clear through the whole countryside. "I'm gonna let it shine."

As they neared him, the hounds passed the visible threshold of the shadow of the censer into the light of the shield. At that instant, their bodies burst into flames. They reared back, desperate to escape the light, but their forward momentum slammed them into Ethan's shield, and they vaporized as the other hounds had.

More determined than ever, Ethan set his sights on the bishop and Mayhem. Darkness would not win.

With a last desperate tug, the bishop pulled the sword from Mayhem's mouth, after which the hound let out a howl and cowered behind the bishop as if to avoid Ethan's approaching light.

"Acolyte!" Desperation swelled the bishop's voice. "We must kill this boy; do you hear me? Take him from the left." He tightened his two-handed grip on the sword he'd just pulled out of Mayhem.

The dandelion acolyte and the bishop, flanking Ethan, edged their way toward him.

Ethan's eyes darted left and right, watching as the bishop and the acolyte feinted this way and that. The little boy pulled his shield out of the ground, first making sure that Aiden and Lauren were still directly in front of him. As he expected, the shield retracted to the size of a buckler. The light shining from the shield also reduced, and under the dark influence of the censor, it was barely enough to light the way to Lauren and Aiden. Still, it was enough.

So far, so good. Ethan took a breath and dashed forward. With the help of the Light, he'd save Lauren and Aiden!

The dandelion acolyte swiped at him as he passed but overreached. Ethan managed to block the blow with a backhanded move of his buckler.

The acolyte's overreach caused him to lose his balance, and he tripped over his own feet. Falling, he dropped his sword.

Seizing the opportunity, Ethan flew past the Acolyte of the Dandelion Order and reached Aiden and Lauren. Then he whirled to face their attackers. As Ethan raised his shield, it transformed to its supernatural size and brightness. He slammed it into the ground, where it was able to stand on its own.

Again, in the face of the light, the Acolyte of the Dandelion Order and the bishop shielded their eyes and wobbled backward.

"Sissy! Aiden!" Ethan shook his sister's shoulders, then his brother's, desperate to rouse them. "Wake up! We have to fight!" At all times, he made sure to stay crouched behind the protection of his shield.

Lauren stirred. Aiden let out a groan.

A sigh escaped Ethan as he watched his siblings sit up and shake their heads to clear them. They'd revived! Encouraged, he again turned his attention to the bishop, who beckoned the Acolyte of the Dandelion Order to come close. Though Ethan could not hear anything, he suspected the bishop was whispering a vile strategy to his partner in evil.

Lauren and Aiden struggled to their feet.

Ethan turned toward them, shouting, "Hurry up! They're going to attack!" He grabbed his shield, again ready to react to anything the enemy had planned.

Lauren nodded and prepared her spear to throw. The blue-green wave of power washed over it, and the spear tip appeared.

The bishop threw back his shoulders and strode toward Ethan while the acolyte veered to Ethan's right. As the bishop came into full view of the light, Ethan saw the evil intent in the hard stare of his squinting eyes. "Mayhem," the bishop commanded as he stepped closer. "Kill the boy! Now!"

The wounded hound looked first at Ethan, then the shield, and sat back on its haunches, shaking its head.

The bishop stopped in his tracks. "How dare you disobey me, you cowardly cur! By the name of Dark One, I say kill the boy!"

Ethan heard the Dandelion Acolyte let out a battle yell, and he poked his head around the shield to see the acolyte rush toward them. Lauren stepped forward, and Ethan saw her grip her spear. The blue-green aura brightened at its tip and narrowed to a pinpoint of light. She hurled it at the acolyte with a grunt of exertion.

The spear tip hit him full in the chest and disappeared, much to Ethan's amazement.

With an awful groan, the Acolyte of the Dandelion Order flew backward, his head thudding against the ground.

The shaft of the spear popped back into Lauren's hand. Ethan saw her bobble the spear for a moment like she wasn't expecting it to pop back into her hand. Then she moved to Ethan's right.

Aiden joined Ethan and Lauren, his sword enveloped in blue-white flames.

Mayhem, still resting on his haunches, seemed to fix his gaze on the blade, then got up to put the bishop between it and the children.

"Children!" Pure fury laced the bishop's voice. "You cannot hope to win. The Darkness will overpower you!"

"I don't think so!" Aiden brandished his sword toward the hellhound, and it continued its retreat. "The Light is stronger."

"Never!" retorted the bishop, creeping forward, his sword gripped so tightly in both hands that his knuckles turned white.

"Oh, yeah?" Aiden made a move for the sack that covered the lantern. "After I uncover this, we'll see who wins."

"No!" The bishop's head swiveled about as if he sought an escape route.

Lauren lifted the spear.

"Mayhem, come! Now!" The bishop looked over his shoulder as he attempted to escape the Light of Lauren's spear. Ethan watched Lauren as she targeted the bishop. Just when she got a bead on the man, he shifted his direction. Lauren took a step forward.

Mayhem howled, then bounded after his master.

His robes flying, the bishop leapt onto Mayhem's back, kicking his heels into the hound's side. The hound and its master hurtled toward the path to the stream faster than any horse he had ever seen. In a few heartbeats, they were down the hill to the creek and utterly hidden in the brush and trees of the surrounding woods.

Aiden grabbed the sack around the lantern and tried to untie the cord that bound it. When it wouldn't budge, he hacked it off with his sword.

Light flooded out of the opened sack. A focused beam of energy shot out of the lantern into the censer, instantly vaporizing it.

After that, the weapons lost their holy light, and the shield returned to the size of a buckler. The exhausted children let their weapons drop from their arms.

Lauren wiped the sweat off her forehead. "It's over."

"Wow, E!" Aiden threw himself into his brother's arms. "You saved us."

Nodding, Lauren joined the hug. "Ethan, you really shone your light, and just when we needed it."

"Aw, thanks, Sissy." His cheeks were warm with embarrassment at how they were fawning all over him.

Ethan ducked his head. "It wasn't me, though, at least not at first. The knight protector told me to shine my light."

"Oh, my goodness!" Lauren clapped her hand to her mouth. "I totally forgot about him. I hope he's OK. I'm sure his hands hurt from the way we tied him up."

"We had to," Ethan said. "We didn't know if he represented the Light or the Darkness."

Aiden nodded.

When they reached the porch, Ethan grabbed Lauren and Aiden by the backs of their shirts. "Wait! We forgot about Brother Flower. Where is he? I lost track of him after the hound attacked him. Is he OK?"

"I don't know." Lauren turned around. Worry creased her forehead. "Let's look for him.

18.   Aftermath

The children retrieved their weapons, just in case evil decided to return, and hurried back into the yard. The Light from the lantern burned so intensely that the glare made it hard to see. Their faces cast downward; they shielded their eyes as they picked their way across the barnyard.

Not far from the barn, they saw a body sprawled on the ground.

It was Brother Flower. Blood pooled around the deep gash in his chest, and he was barely breathing.

"Brother Flower!" Ethan stumbled forward, nearly collapsing by the side of his fallen friend. "Sissy, quick! He's hurt! Help him!"

Aiden and Lauren rushed to Brother Flower's side. His breath came in ragged gasps and blood-soaked his torn purple robe.

He had once been so proud of that robe.

"Aiden!" Lauren swallowed tears. "Go untie the knight protector. Maybe he can help." Even as she spoke, deep down, she knew there was no help short of a miracle.

Lauren followed Aiden as he rushed inside with his sword.

"Boy! What are you doing with that sword?" The knight protector was still bound to the table leg, a concerned look on his face.

"Letting you out." Aiden cut away the ropes holding the knight protector. "We need help. Brother Flower got hurt trying to save us!"

The knight protector's skin sagged about his eyes. "What happened with the bishop?" He struggled to his feet, keeping his palms flat on the tabletop as if to steady himself. He looked as if he'd aged a decade in the last hour.

"He got away, but the Y'lohnu Censer was destroyed," Aiden answered.

The knight protector's countenance lightened. He massaged his hands, then raised them toward the ceiling as if in prayer.

"We don't have time to talk now, sir." Aiden gently but firmly took hold of the knight protector's arm. "Brother Flower needs our help."

Lauren had already grabbed towels and a bucket of water. Aiden took hold of the knight protector and guided him outside.

Kneeling next to the stricken Brother Flower, Ethan sobbed inconsolably.

Aiden felt his lip tremble as they neared the scene.

"Brother Flower!" Lauren kneeled and curled her legs underneath her as she cradled his head in her hands. "Can you hear me?"

"Yes," he managed, his words bubbling out with bloody sputum.

Aiden wished the knight protector would hurry. Brother Flower needed their help.

"Brother," Lauren started as she stroked his hair. "Your wounds are grave. I don't think there's anything we can do except pray."

"I feel such pain." A cough tore through a faint whisper, making him hard to understand. "Call ... call me

Nicholas. That's my given name. I … I no longer serve what I now know was the Darkness."

The knight protector, still supported by Aiden, came near and visibly winced at the scene as he managed to kneel on one knee and put his arm around Ethan, whose sobs had not diminished. "Son, the acolyte is not long for this world."

"His name is Nicholas," Lauren said solemnly.

"The only hope for Nicholas now is God's mercy," said the knight protector.

"OK." Ethan wiped away tears and sat straighter. "Let's pray." He bowed his head; the others did the same. "Dear God, please help Nicholas." As he prayed, sniffles punctuated his words. "Please, please fix him, God. He is a good friend, and he saved Sissy and Aiden. He saved Sparkle Frog. He saved me, too." Please, God!" Ethan's voice rang out with the depth and confidence of the young child of faith that he was. "Please save Nicholas."

The Lantern of Light grew brighter, and a light haloed Nicholas's head.

"I have been saved … from the Darkness. You, children, have shown me the Light." Nicholas spoke with clarity, the winces and sighs of pain seemingly gone. "Goodbye, my friends." Nicholas' breath rattled in his chest, which made a great heave, then stilled.

Brother Flower, Nicholas, had breathed his last.

"No! God, please bring him back!" Ethan banged his fist against muddy sod. "He's our friend!" he wailed. "God! Please!"

Lauren and Aiden took a position on each side of their brother and pulled him close. Huddled together, they wept

and cried out, "He was our friend. He cared. He really did."
Words came out in bits and phrases. They cried tears not
only of the brokenhearted but of those who had known
grave danger and learned hard truths.

As they grieved, the knight protector selected the
largest towel from the pile Aiden had brought, covered
Nicholas's fatal wound, and with a gentleness they didn't
expect from this hard old man, closed Nicholas's eyes.

Then the knight protector took a smaller towel and
wiped his eyes, picked up the Lantern of Light, hobbled
toward the stairs of the Tower of Light, and began the steep
climb.

Soon the Lantern of Light again hung in its proper
position and beamed with an awesome radiance across the
Heathlands.

The knight protector returned and knelt by the still-
grieving children, saying, "Children, you indeed witnessed
a tragedy, but I need you to pull yourselves together, not
for my sake but for Nicholas's."

One by one, the children raised their heads. Finally,
Lauren nodded.

"Young girl, will you get a blanket? We need to remove
him from the yard. He will be protected tonight in the
Tower of Light." He looked toward the heavens.
"Tomorrow, we will give him a proper burial."

With a nod, Lauren rose, went inside, and got a linen
sheet, one of their best. She laid it out on the ground next to
Nicholas's body and helped the knight protector move the
body onto it.

Finally, they laid him on the floor of the Tower of Light. The children formed a huddle, and their tears returned, though with less intensity than before.

When they quieted, the knight protector stepped close. "Children, you are safe. Your faith has protected you and guided you to a great victory over evil. The forces of darkness have been sent running, and an object of great evil has been destroyed."

"Wait!" Aiden broke from the huddle. "The dandelion acolyte is here somewhere."

They set off together, the knight protector limping behind them. Wary of attack, they stayed together. With the aid of the lantern, they could see far across the land.

Aiden turned to the east.

Something yellow-hued caught his eye. It was the robe of the acolyte. Next to his clothes, in a low area, was the knight protector's sword.

"Whoa!" Aiden put his hand to his chest. "Did the Light destroy him, too?"

Lauren, who'd come up beside her brother, pointed at the ground. "No, I don't think so." She frowned. "Footprints."

Ethan joined Lauren and Aiden. "I think the Light made him remember who he really was, too, like when Sissy hit Nicholas, so maybe now he'll join the forces of good."

Aiden put an arm around Ethan's shoulder. "I bet you are right. To make sure, should we track him down?"

The knight protector shook his head. "I don't believe he will cause any more trouble. He has no weapons and apparently no more loyalty to the Darkness. You all have done well protecting the Tower of Light. Your parents would be proud."

The knight protector guided the children toward the house. "In the morning, I will begin the work required to place a proper garrison around the tower and ensure its safety." He patted each child on the head in a tender and loving way. "As for the three of you, you have earned a rest. Come along. Let's get you to bed."

The children retrieved their weapons and slowly walked back to the house. Lauren did her best to make sure they tracked in as little mud as possible. Lauren and Ethan went up the ladder to the loft as Aiden stoked the fire.

The knight protector bolted the doors, and Aiden saw him take a seat in the great room in Father's chair. He picked up the Good Book to read as Aiden climbed the stairs. For the first time in days, Aiden felt they were going to sleep safely through the night.

19. Epilogue

The children slept more deeply than they had since their mother left. Sunrise came, but they did not wake as usual due to the sheer exhaustion from the previous day's battle. However, as the sun rose, a warm sunbeam danced on Ethan's head.

He tried to rouse but could not, and realized that somehow, he was not in his bedroom but instead in a strange place, a dark place.

Black cloth walls, like those of a tent, made up the room. There were dark rugs on the ground. In a corner, slumped against a pile of furs, sat Mother. She wore an elegant black dress.

Mother! Ethan stretched his neck, desperate to get a closer look. He blinked, then squinted.

A single dim light had its source from a gap at the top of the tent. The light hit the wall just above Mother's head. Mother stirred slightly and sat up.

The beam of light hit her forehead.

Mother's eyes opened, and she seemed to be looking straight into Ethan's eyes.

"Ethan, your light is so very bright." Tears rolled down her lovely face, and she began to cry. "I saw it last night! It was so glorious and undoubtedly cause for celebration, but you must not tarry at home. You must take your light to the far corners of the land and light the other towers.

"The forces of Darkness are after you!" Mother continued. "Their lord, the Dark One, comes again for you. Seek help from the knight protector. Father shared his plans to shine the Light from Blooming Glen with him." Her eyes glistened like they held diamonds; so brilliant were her tears. "You must shine your light over the whole wide world! Let it shine."

A shadow passed over the beam of light: Mother was gone. Ethan now saw an image of a man in a cage wearing an iron mask. He was bound to the bars with iron restraints. Ethan began to shake. Despite the cover, Ethan knew precisely who he was: their father.

"Daddy! I'll shine my light and save you!" Ethan pleaded with the darkness, "Sissy, Aiden, and me will shine our light over the whole, wide world."

...to be continued in Still Small Voice

If you enjoyed Light of Mine please share your review

Good Reads   Amazon.com

Reading Comprehension Questions

The answer key and free digital download of the unit study are available at
https://towersoflight.net/homeschool

1. The Tower of Light	
Why does the Father build the tower?	
What special animals visits the farm?	
What does The Father do for work?	
Are the Mighty Mercenaries trustworthy? Why or why not?	
Where does the light for the tower come from?	

2. Tragedy Strikes	
What does the Mother do during the storm?	
What makes Aiden think the windmill came down from lightning?	
Why did Aiden think the Dark One was responsible for the broken windmill?	
What does Mother realize may have led to Father's disappearance?	
Who does Mother say will help the children?	

3. Life Endures	
What did Lauren use to organize the work?	
Who is Ethan's special friend?	
What little accomplishment made Ethan very proud?	
How did Lauren react to the fire being put out?	

4. The Visitor

Who is Aiden's special friend?	
Who comes to visit the children?	
Who was supposed to visit the children?	
What tool does Aiden use to fix the windmill?	
What is the theme of the stories Lauren reads in the Good Book?	

5. The Discovery

Where was Lauren in her Dream?	
Why was Lauren concerned with cleaning up the great room?	
What do the kids find in the sack? Why is it special?	

6. What is Truth?

What does Sparkle Frog do that's so amazing?	
How are the children treated after church?	
What item is sent with the children?	
What document is shown to the children? Where did it come from?	
Who returns home with the children?	

7. A Stranger at Church

Why are the kids excited to see the Parson?	
What stands out about the countryside on the way to the church?	
Why was Ethan acting strange when he returned?	
Who storms out of the church and why?	

8. Honoring the Sabbath	
What did the acolyte not know about the Light?	
What did the acolyte want for lunch, and why did it surprise the children?	
What does Meow Meow decide to play with?	
Why did the Acolyte apologize?	

9. The Acolyte of the Violet Order	
What does the sky look like on the way home? Why does that matter?	
What does the Acolyte think of the Parson?	
How does the Acolyte react to meeting Daddy Duck the first time?	
What happened to the tower while the children were gone?	

10. Dark Water

What does the Acolyte save Ethan from?	
What do the children do to fix Sparkle Frog? Why is the Acolyte surprised?	
What do the kids see the Knight Protector doing?	
What happens to the horn of power?	
Why does the Acolyte make them go home?	

11. Father's Instructions

What do the children bring to the Acolyte?	
Who visited the house and why?	
What got added to the tower?	

12. Finding the Source	
What wakes the children up?	
Where does the quest for the source of the dark water take the children?	
What do the children find there?	
What amazing things happen to destroy the darkness?	
Who do the children see as they flee?	

13. The Struggle for the Light	
What happens when Lauren uses her spear?	
What happens to the Knight Protector?	
What do the kids find in the tower?	

What does Ethan find along the way?	

14. Laying the Trap

What do they decide to do about the Knight Protector?	
Describe the trap the children set up.	

15. The Acolyte Awakens

Who visits the children and why?	
How do they get rid of the Acolyte's head egg?	
What is wrong with the Acolyte when he wakes?	

16. Like a Moth to the Flame

Did the children's trap work? Who got caught in it?	
What does the Acolyte want to do about the Knight?	
What heroic act does Ethan do?	
How does the Knight explain his behavior?	
What happens when the acolyte blows his horn?	

17. Let it Shine

What advice does the Knight give Ethan? Why is that advice special to Ethan?	
What happens when the Acolyte attempts to help the kids?	
What does the Holy Spirit's power allow their weapons to do?	
Is the Censor more powerful than the lantern?	

What happens to the Bishop?	

18. Aftermath

What did the children do to help the acolyte? Did it work? Why or why not?	

19. Epilogue

Where was Mother?	

About the Author

Allen Brokken is a teacher at heart, a husband, and a father most of all. He's a joyful writer by the abundant grace of God. He began writing the Towers of Light series for his own children to help him illustrate the deep truths of the Bible in an engaging and age-appropriate way. He's dedicated 15 years of his life to volunteer roles in children's ministry and youth development.

Now that his own children are off to college, he's sharing his life experiences on social media, at home school conferences, and through his blog, occasional cool dad projects, and the Silly Celebrations newsletter at https://towersoflight.net/subscribe

You can get sneak peeks of the ongoing adventures of Lauren, Aiden, and Ethan (plus their pets!) regularly and the #dadjokeoftheday on all the major social media platforms.
@allenbrokkenauthor

Towers of Light Series

The series insightfully examines Christian values from the perspective of three small children facing insurmountable problems and succeeding by faith and grace alone.

Book 1: *Light of Mine*- *Discernment*
The Darkness has taken their parents. Can Lauren, Aiden, and Ethan discern who to trust before it takes them too?

Book 2: *Still Small Voice* – *Conscience*
Lauren, Aiden, and Ethan want to follow their conscience to save their parents, but their Uncle has other plans. Will he see the light before it's too late?

Book 3: *Fear No Evil* -*Courage*
Lost and alone in a valley of Darkness, will Lauren, Aiden, and Ethan find God's courage to find redemption and each other?

Book 4: *Armor of God* – *Faith*
Lauren, Aiden, and Ethan race across the Heathlands on a quest to arm themselves with the Armor of God. Will their faith give them the power to save their father?

Book 5: *Wellspring of Life* – *Redemption*
Lauren, Aiden, and Ethan must find the legendary wellspring of life. Will they be able to share its living waters before it's too late?

Book 6: *Demolishing the Stronghold* – *Victory*
Lauren, Aiden, and Ethan reach Blooming Glen only to find the city defended by the Dark One's Forces. Will they have the faith to overcome the enemy and Light the Tower?

Want to have another adventure in new amazing places?

A twelve-year-old girl discovers a link between the father she's never known and a mysterious shop where the snow globes open portals to other worlds. An adventurous science fantasy for readers who like to explore.

"Snow Globe Travelers: Samuel's Legacy will appeal to science fantasy lovers of all ages, and it's most highly recommended."
     —READERS' FAVORITE, A FIVE-STAR REVIEW

Looking for quality literature for language arts?

New Classics Study Guides

offers free literature units for homeschooling. This is a curated collection chosen by a veteran homeschool curriculum provider, Phyllis Wheeler of MotherBoardBooks.com. The authors have banded together and created study guides for their books. Explore the links to find your next new classic for your child's literature unit. Download for free!

newclassicsstudyguides.com

Made in the USA
Columbia, SC
28 April 2023

15718902R00138